HERGÉ

★

THE ADVENTURES OF
TINTIN

★

THE RED SEA SHARKS

LITTLE, BROWN AND COMPANY
New York ∿ Boston

Little, Brown Books for Young Readers

Hachette Book Group
237 Park Avenue, New York, NY 10017
Visit our Web site at www.lb-kids.com

Little, Brown Books for Young Readers is a division of
Hachette Book Group, Inc.
The Little, Brown name and logo are trademarks of
Hachette Book Group, Inc.

First Paperback Edition: September 1976

Library of Congress catalog card no. 76-13278
ISBN: 978-0-316-35848-4
30 29 28 27 26 25 24 23 22
Published pursuant to agreement with Casterman, Paris
Not for sale in the British Commonwealth
Printed in China

THE RED SEA SHARKS

One evening, at the cinema . . .

THE END

Did you enjoy the film, Captain?

Oh yes . . . so-so, so-so.

The chap who played the lead is a good actor . . .

He looks like Alcazar; don't you think so?

. . . but the end was too improbable. The old uncle hasn't seen his nephew for twenty years . . . he starts thinking about him . . . the door opens, and hey-presto, who's there? The nephew!

It's as if I was thinking of . . . I don't know, someone or other . . .

For example, take General Alcazar, whom you mentioned just now. He completely vanished from our lives years ago . . .

Well, d'you suppose, if I just think about him he'll pop up on the street corner, like that, bingo!?

!

Look here, you misguided missile, you! Can't you watch where you're going?

It's GENERAL ALCAZAR!

Caramba!

It's extraordinary! Imagine! The Captain and I were just this moment talking about you!

Qué? . . . Of me?

Yes, of you . . . weren't we, Captain? Then up you pop like a jack-in-a-box. It's incredible . . . But tell me, General, what are you doing nowadays?

Me? . . . Er . . . Well . . . Si . . . I . . . travel . . . But . . .

Por favor . . . excuse please . . . In mucho hurry . . . Already late for appointment . . . I go now.

Oh, what a pity . . . At all events, here's my address. And where can we find you, General?

Er . . . Um . . . At thees hotel . . . er . . . thees Hotel Bristol.

Good! The Bristol . . . And when do you . . .

Just so . . . Now I go . . . Adios, amigos!

Goodbye, General.

Well, well! Frankly, I don't think your friend Alcazar was in a very chatty mood!

Yes, an odd fellow. Oh well, come on.

? OH!

Crumbs! It's the general's wallet. He didn't put it right inside his pocket.

Quick! He can't have got far.

Hello, where's he gone to? . . .

Perhaps he got into a car . . . Never mind. The Hotel Bristol is quite near; we'll leave his wallet there.

A few minutes later, at the Bristol . . .

General Alcazar? . . . No, Sir, we have no one of that name here.

I wonder: perhaps he's registered under another name . . . Ramon Zarate? . . .

Ramon Zarate? . . . No, sir. A Spanish gentleman?

South American. Quite well-built. A long chin . . . small moustache . . . Wait, I'll try to draw him for you.

There . . . That's about it . . .

No, sir. I'm terribly sorry, but I don't know the gentleman.

Oh? That's odd. Well, thank you.

Now what can we do to return that idiot's wallet to him?

That's what I'm wondering.

I say, why shouldn't the wallet itself give us a clue towards finding the general. Come on; we'll go in here.

Bring us . . . er . . . let's see . . . let's see . . .

Two glasses of ginger beer.

Now then, let's see what's inside here.

ROSSINI

Pound notes, French and Belgian money, a hotel bill, a four-leaf clover, a lottery ticket from San Theodoros . . . in fact, nothing to give us a lead.

. . . And in this envelope, photos of aircraft . . . Odd, isn't it, Captain?

Ah, a letter! . . . This time I think we're on to something. Look, Captain.

Friday

Dear Sir,

Please telephone PIC 8524 between 10. and 12.0 p.m. Ask for Mr. Debrett

Regards,
J.D.M.C.

But the general's address isn't here.

I know, but I'll ring up the number given in the letter.

ROSSINI

Hello, is that PIC 8524? May I speak to Mr Debrett? . . . Who am I? . . . A friend of General Alcazar, and I . . . Hello? . . . HELLO?? . . .

Can you hear me? . . . What? . . . You don't know the name Alcazar? . . . What about Ramon Zarate? . . . Nor that? . . . You see, sir, I found his wallet and . . . I beg your pardon?

I tell you, sir, I am not Mr Debrett! I don't know your General Alhambra, and I am not interested in your story . . . Goodbye!

There's politeness for you! . . .

Very odd . . . They don't know of him at that number. Too bad . . . We'd better be getting home to Marlinspike.

A little later . . .
How strange. The front door's open . . .

WOOAAAH! . . . WOOAAAH! . . .
? ?

Good heavens! My poor Snowy! Who's done this to you?!

I'll get to the bottom of it!

Hey, Captain, what's happened to you?

Billions of blue blistering barnacles! Who's the thundering son of a sea-gherkin who did that? . . . Nestor! . . . Nestor!

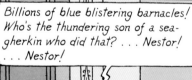
HAAAAH! . . .

Th . . . th . . . th . . . there behind you!

RRHOAH! . . .

4

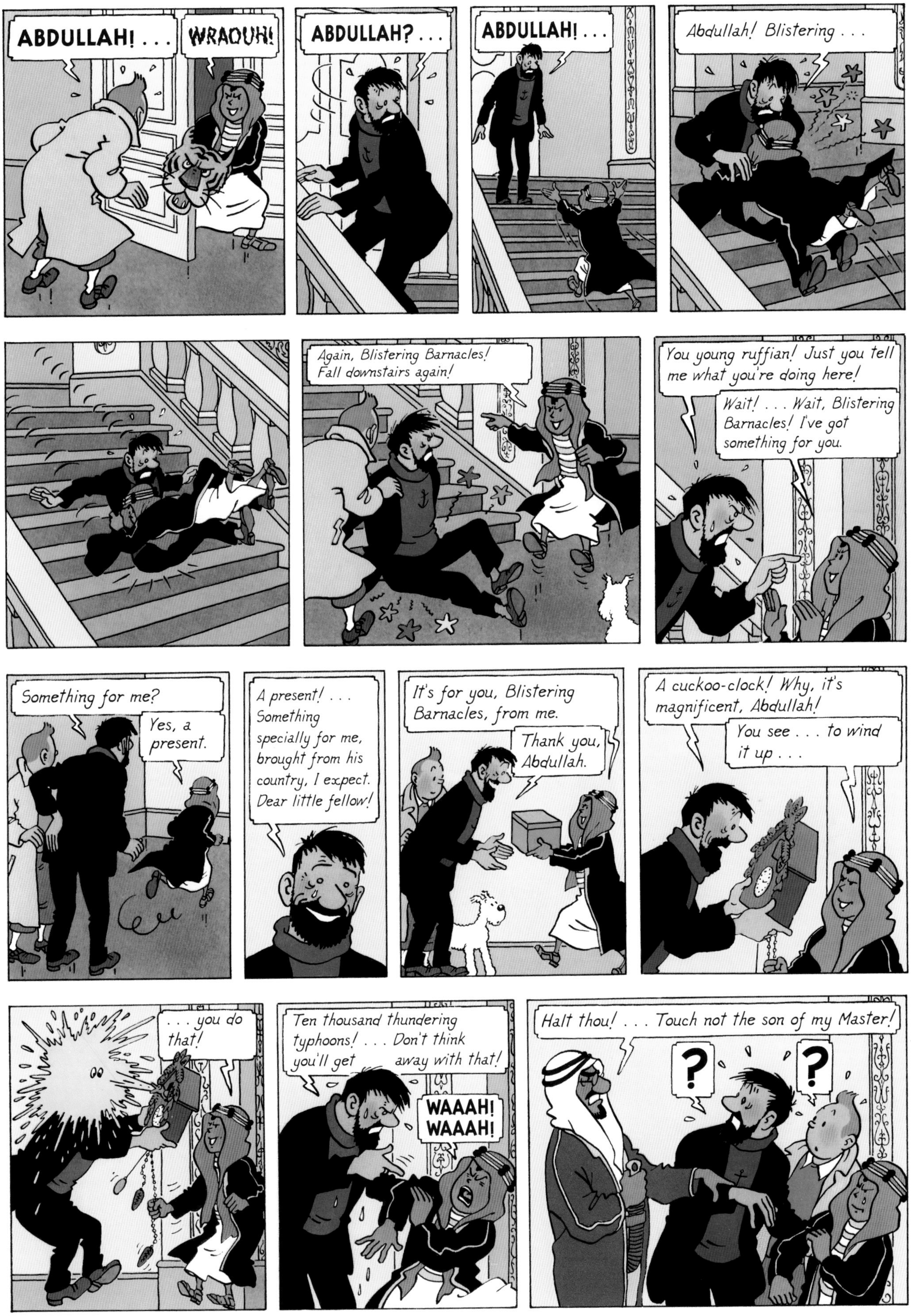
ABDULLAH! . . .
WRAOUH!
ABDULLAH? . . .
ABDULLAH! . . .
Abdullah! Blistering . . .
Again, Blistering Barnacles! Fall downstairs again!
You young ruffian! Just you tell me what you're doing here!
Wait! . . . Wait, Blistering Barnacles! I've got something for you.
Something for me?
Yes, a present.
A present! . . . Something specially for me, brought from his country, I expect. Dear little fellow!
It's for you, Blistering Barnacles, from me.
Thank you, Abdullah.
A cuckoo-clock! Why, it's magnificent, Abdullah!
You see . . . to wind it up . . .
. . . you do that!
Ten thousand thundering typhoons! . . . Don't think you'll get away with that!
WAAAH! WAAAH!
Halt thou! . . . Touch not the son of my Master!
?
?

Me Hassim, servant to His Highness Prince Abdullah . . .

And I bring you message from my Master.

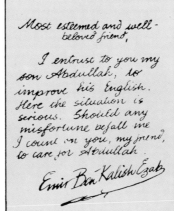

Most esteemed and well-beloved friend,

I entrust to you my son Abdullah, to improve his English. Here the situation is serious. Should any misfortune befall me I count on you, my friend, to care for Abdullah.

Emir Ben Kalish Ezab

Read that, Tintin, it's for you . . . Tell me Hassim, what does the Emir mean . . . "the situation is serious"?

I know not, Effendi.

What d'you make of it? One thing's clear: we've got Abdullah on our hands. We'll have to bring the young scamp to heel.

Abdullah! . . . You little brat! I'm going to teach you a lesson . . .

WAAH!

Halt thou! . . . Touch not the son of my Master!

Touch not! Touch not! You arabesque, you! D'you imagine I'm going to let that little pest raise Cain in my house?

Just wait till I find you, you young rapscallion!

Oh sir! . . . Sir! . . . It's terrible, sir . . . All those foreign persons have settled themselves . . .

Later, Nestor . . . tell me later.

. . . in the state-rooms!

The next morning . . .

RRRRING
RRRRING
?

HELLO?

Blue blistering barnacles in a thundering typhoon!

All right . . . All right! . . . I'm coming!

RRRING
RRRING

RRRING

Hello? . . . Hello? . . . Who? . . . What? . . . Who d'you want?! No, Madam. I am not Mr Cutts the butcher!

☆!!!+ ◎ ♪ ★ ☀ ≶ ☀ ! >><☆ ♏♏ !

BLUB BLUB
BLUB
BLUB SPLOSH

RRRING

!?

No answer? . . . I suppose they're all asleep still . . .

To be precise, I'd say . . .

HELLO!

Hello? . . . Who's that? Thompson? . . . What? . . . Oh yes, with a "p". Well?

I . . . I . . . I'm not disturbing you, am I?

Er . . . not in the least. Go on . . .

Is Tintin here this morning? . . . Yes. You'd like to speak to him? . . . Right . . . What? . . . Do we know General Alcazar? . . . Yes, why?

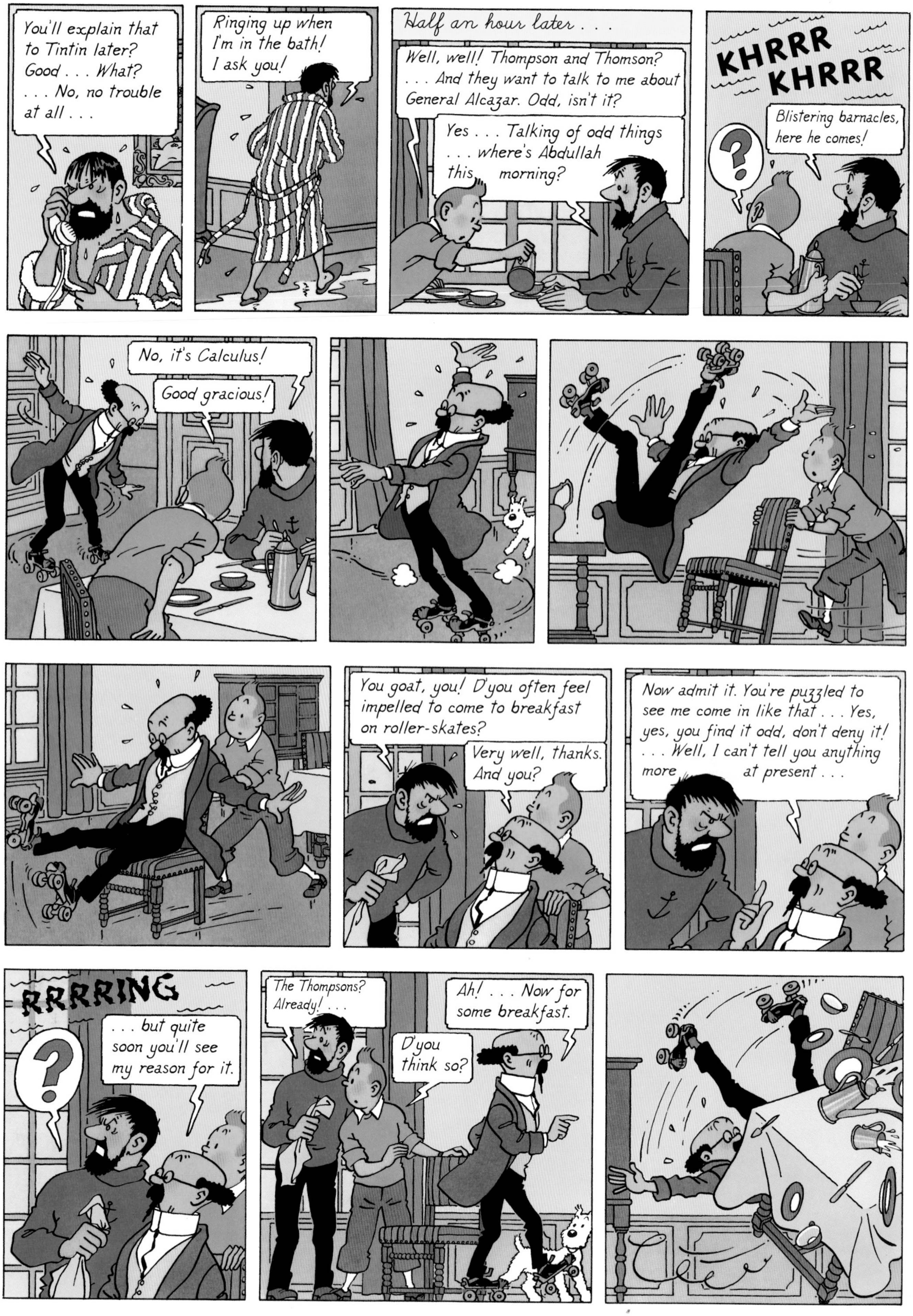
You'll explain that to Tintin later? Good . . . What? . . . No, no trouble at all . . .
Ringing up when I'm in the bath! I ask you!
Half an hour later . . .
Well, well! Thompson and Thomson? . . . And they want to talk to me about General Alcazar. Odd, isn't it?
Yes . . . Talking of odd things . . . where's Abdullah this morning?
KHRRR KHRRR
Blistering barnacles, here he comes!
?
No, it's Calculus!
Good gracious!
You goat, you! D'you often feel impelled to come to breakfast on roller-skates?
Very well, thanks. And you?
Now admit it. You're puzzled to see me come in like that . . . Yes, yes, you find it odd, don't deny it! . . . Well, I can't tell you anything more at present . . .
RRRRING
. . . but quite soon you'll see my reason for it.
?
The Thompsons? Already! . . .
Ah! . . . Now for some breakfast.
D'you think so?

RRRRING BANG

You thundering nitwitted numbskull you! Haven't you finished acting the goat yet?

Who rang, Nestor?

I found no one the first time, sir. But the second time, I saw Abdullah running away.

RRRING

I bet that's him! But he won't get away with it this time. Nestor, go and bring the hose-pipe!

Now . . . as soon as he rings, you open the door, and then: psshhtt! . . . We'll get a good laugh!

RRING

That's it! . . . Quick, open up, Nestor!

I . . . I'm dreadfully sorry! . . . Please forgive me! You see, it's Abdullah's fault. The young rapscallion kept ringing the bell . . .

Ha! ha! ha! ha!

?

A few minutes later . . .

Well, here's the position. Interpol have asked us to keep an eye on a man called Dawson, and to collect all the information we can about his activities . . .

. . . and also about the people he meets. It so happens that you know one of them: General Alcazar. What can you tell us about him?

Very little, as a matter of fact.

I knew him when he was President of the Republic of San Theodoros. I met him later, in Europe. He'd been deposed by his rival, General Tapioca, and had fled from his country. He'd become a knife-thrower on the music-halls . . . That's all.

All? Really? And what did he say to you, when you met him last night?

?

Aha! That surprised you, eh? You forget, my friend, in our job there's nothing we don't know.

To be precise: we know nothing in our job!

It's true that we met him last night. I was going to tell you . . . He said he was travelling, he was in a hurry, and he was staying at the Hotel . . . er . . . the Hotel . . .

Excelsior; yes, we know.

Oh? Well, that's the lot . . . He didn't say anything else . . . But what have you against him? What do you suspect?

Why are we suspect? I mean, what do we suspect? My dear fellow, if you imagine we'll tell you he's smuggling aircraft, you're much mistaken. "Mum's the word", that's our motto.

Well said! . . . To be precise: "Dumb's the word", that's our motto. The general may have come to Europe to buy up old aircraft, but you won't learn that from us! Now we must be going. Goodbye, Tintin.

Goodbye.

Ah! Here comes Nestor with our hats and sticks.

What a very peculiar thing: my hat has shrunk.

How strange. With me it's the opposite; I've got a swollen head . . .

Oh, I see. We've got muddled up. You have my hat and I have yours.

That's it: our mats are in a huddle. In short, we're contrarywise . . .

But it still isn't right!

Nor is mine!

May I see? . . . You can bet Abdullah's behind this . . .

Abdullalah?

There! . . . I thought as much. It's an old joke: newspapers folded up and slipped into the band.

A little later on . . .

Abdullah and his tricks!

Well, what did our Siamese twins want?

Just read this advertisement I've found in an old newspaper!

FOR SALE
AIRCRAFT, TANKS, SUBMARINES ETC
Further particulars from J.D.M.C., Box No. 5083, DR
EXPORT CO. LTD.

Extraordinary! . . . Why don't they add: "on easy terms". You'll see, we'll end up buying a battleship or the 'Queen Mary' on the never-never!

Maybe. But did you notice the initials?

J.D.M.C. . . . J.D.M.C. . . . Thundering typhoons! Alcazar's wallet! The signature on that letter!

Precisely!

No doubt about it: the general's here to buy armaments. But that's no reason for failing to return his wallet. And since Thompson and Thomson have kindly told us the right address . . .

I'll come with you.

Later, at the Hotel Excelsior . . .

General Alcazar? Yes, he's here, sir. I just saw him go past. You'll find him in the lounge.

Thank you.

There . . .

Look . . . he's talking to someone. But . . . good heavens! It's Dawson. I've met him before. He was police chief in the International Settlement in Shanghai.

And there in the background, lurking behind their newspapers . . .

The Thompsons!

This all looks pretty fishy; I'd like to know a bit more about it. Listen, Captain; you stay here, and as soon as Dawson goes, you return General Alcazar's wallet. I'll follow Dawson. We'll meet at Marlinspike.

OK

An hour later . . .

There he is . . . getting into that black Jaguar.

Quick, taxi! . . . Follow that black Jaguar, there, ahead of us.

Where are we off to now?

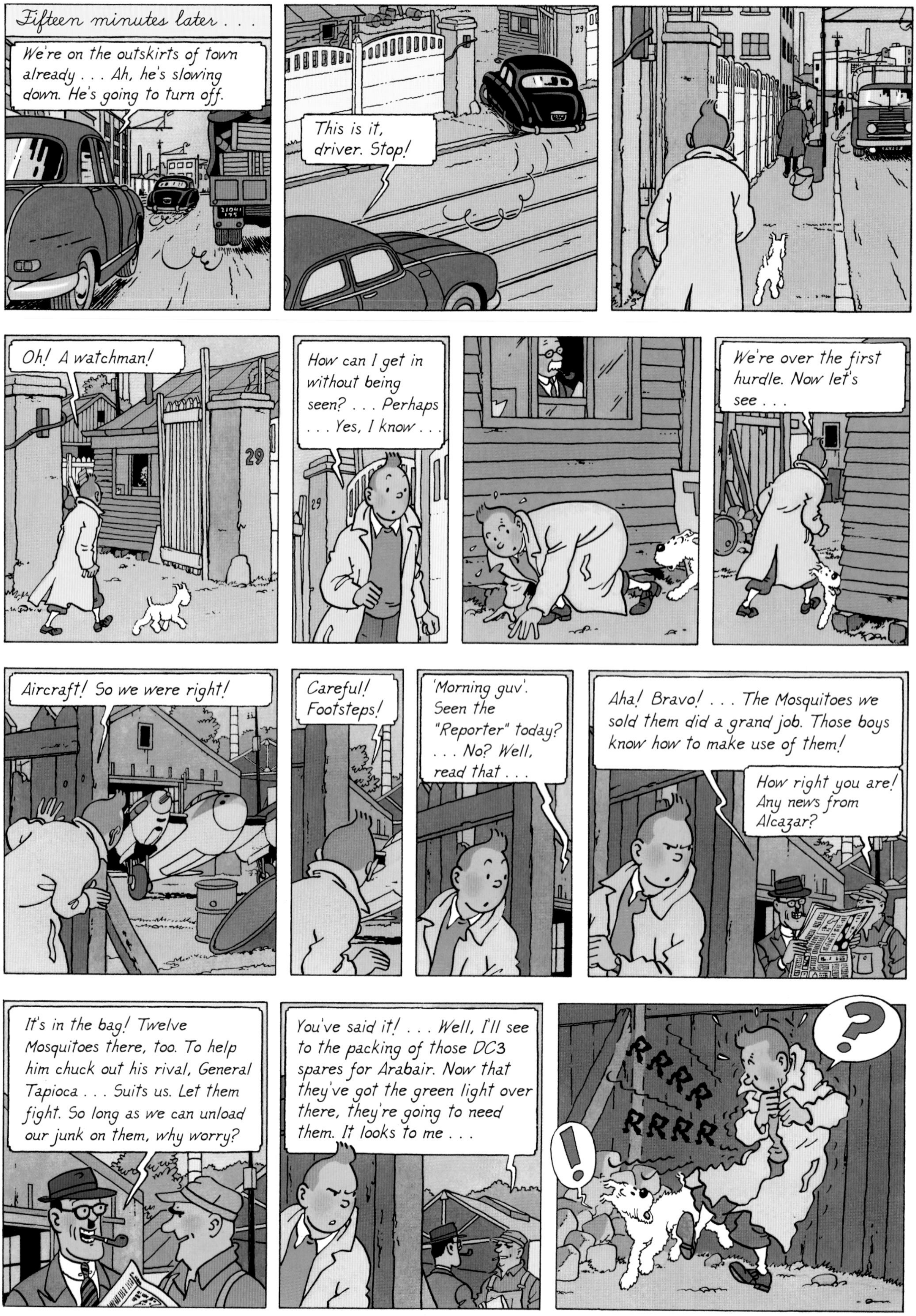
Fifteen minutes later . . .
We're on the outskirts of town already . . . Ah, he's slowing down. He's going to turn off.
This is it, driver. Stop!
Oh! A watchman!
How can I get in without being seen? . . . Perhaps . . . Yes, I know . . .
We're over the first hurdle. Now let's see . . .
Aircraft! So we were right!
Careful! Footsteps!
'Morning guv'. Seen the "Reporter" today? . . . No? Well, read that . . .
Aha! Bravo! . . . The Mosquitoes we sold them did a grand job. Those boys know how to make use of them!
How right you are! Any news from Alcazar?
It's in the bag! Twelve Mosquitoes there, too. To help him chuck out his rival, General Tapioca . . . Suits us. Let them fight. So long as we can unload our junk on them, why worry?
You've said it! . . . Well, I'll see to the packing of those DC3 spares for Arabair. Now that they've got the green light over there, they're going to need them. It looks to me . . .
RRRR RRRR
?
!

What's that? . . . What on earth's going on? . . . What's this confounded thing?

Where the devil's that row coming from?!

An alarm-clock!

Abdullah, the little pest! I'll bet he put that alarm-clock in my pocket!

A young lad with a white dog, you say? . . . How did they manage to get in without your seeing?

"Daily Reporter" sir . . .

Thanks.

CRUMBS!

Great Scot! What will the Captain think of this?

A little later . . .

Abdullah! Just you wait till I catch you!

Ha! ha! ha! ha!

Poor kid, all the same. He's too young to realise how serious things are.

BANG

?!!

Blue blistering barnacles! This time I've had enough! . . . The little pest! A firework under my chair while I was having forty winks. It's the end! He's going back to his father!

Too late! . . . Read this . . .

COUP D'ÉTAT IN KHEMED

Wadesdah in Rebel Hands

AIR POWER
ENSURES
REBEL VICTORY

Aircraft Riddle:
Who supplied the
Mosquitoes?

Emir Ben Ka
prisoner of

Bab El Ehr
has seized power.

Special Correspondent in Beirut. Tues
. . . played by the rebel ai
. . . ded the pri

Thundering typhoons! The poor Emir! This explains the serious situation he mentioned in his letter . . . Well, you're right: we can't send Abdullah home.

No, but . . .

. . . perhaps there's another way out. If we can't send him off, there's nothing to stop us going away ourselves.

Tintin, you're a genius. But . . . where can we go?

Where? . . . Well, what about Khemed?

That's it! Khemed . . . Good idea!

What? Khemed? In the middle of a revolution! You're crazy! . . . What could we do there?

Perhaps we might try to rescue the Emir. At the same time, we could try to clear up this odd business of the aircraft.

No, thanks, not for me! . . . You go if you like . . . I'm staying here!

BANG

All right, I'm coming.

A youngster with a white dog? That reminds me of something . . . but what?

RRRING RRRING

Hello? . . . Who's that? . . . Oh, it's you, General . . . What? . . . Oh, your wallet . . . You've got it back?

Yes, they bring him back. This Captain Haddock, who I meet yesterday with one of my friends . . . Tintin . . . Qué? . . . Si, Tintin. You know him? . . . Qué? The telephone call you receive last night? . . . Yes, it was him. He find your number in my wallet.

Tintin! . . . So he's the one sticking his nose into my business! . . . I'll soon take care of him . . .

The airport at Wadesdah, capital of Khemed, three days later . . .

Here comes the plane from Beirut.

You understand? If he's aboard, you put this briefcase in the baggage compartment.

I'm not sorry to get here . . . With these old crates you can never be sure . . .

I say, have you noticed? . . . Armed men all over the place.

Passports, please gentlemen.

I am sorry, gentlemen: you have no permit to stay in Khemed. You must reboard the plane, and return to Beirut.

(15)

Blistering barnacles! What sort of a yarn is that?

Here are your passports. You will be conducted to the aircraft.

Thundering typhoons! You're not getting away with this! Our passports are perfectly in order . . . You have no right . . .

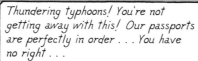

اذهبوا اقشوا دنئة الشصين

Billions of blistering barnacles! To have come so far, and then be held up by these Bashi-bazouks! It's absolutely infuriating!

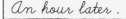

An hour later . . .

There they go! In an hour they'll be flying over the mountains . . . Jebel Kadheh . . . Then . . .

Another eternity in this flying coffin! . . . And a bumpy trip into the bargain. Rattled about like dice in a box . . . I just wonder what sort of trouble will drop on us next.

Thundering typhoons! Why does everything happen to me?

Look out, Captain!

Another . . .

. . . air-pocket!

You're not hurt, are you?

Not at all. I'm just enjoying the luxurious comfort of air travel!

TICK TOCK TICK TOCK TICK TOCK

Golly! I can smell trouble. There's something sinister going on here. I must warn Tintin at once.

I'm wondering WHO warned the authorities at Wadesdah of our arrival, and WHO persuaded them to deport us?

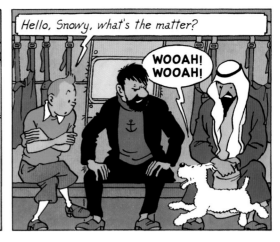

Hello, Snowy, what's the matter?

WOOAH! WOOAH!

Here, will you stop that! You know, he . . . yes, he wants to show me something. All right, I'll follow you . . .

WOOAH! WOOAH!

In there? It's the luggage. You want me to go in? All right, I'm coming.

WOOAH! WOOAH!

PH-E-E-E-T

?

PH-E-E-E-T

What's that siren for?

الخطر يبقه

An engine on fire! That's the alarm for the extinguishers!

Thundering typhoons! The extinguishers haven't worked; it's burning more fiercely than ever!

Wadesdah Tower . . . Wadesdah Tower . . . This is KH-OZD . . . Starboard motor on fire . . . Extinguishers unserviceable. We're turning back . . . We'll try to reach Wadesdah.

It's no good! It's too heavy. I shall just have to . . .

TOCK
TICK
TICK
TOCK
TICK TOCK

This is KH-OZD . . . Starboard engine still burning . . . Port engine misfiring . . . We are losing height . . .

I simply must make him understand. He's got to come and look at this thing.

Again? . . . No, old chap, that's enough. I tell you, this is no time for games.

A parachute . . . I insist that you give me a parachute!

Why won't you come and look!

Don't lose your head, sir. You'd find a parachute quite useless now . . .

I want a parachute, I tell you! I've paid for my seat, and . . .

Look here, young fellow, keep calm, will you? And leave the pilot alone: he's got enough on his plate already!

I'm sorry about this, but . . .

Good lad! . . . Thanks! Everybody hang on tight, we're going to try to land . . .

This is KH-OZD . . . We're over the southern edge of the Kadheh . . . We've jettisoned the fuel . . . We're stopping the port motor . . . We're trying a belly landing.

Allah be praised! . . .
We are safe!

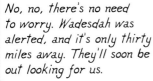

Whew! that's it!
The fire is out.

Don't stay here in the open
sun. We'd better move into the
shadow of those rocks, while
we wait for a rescue party.

Come out of there,
Snowy! At once!

Wooah!
Wooah!

Wooah!
Wooah!

No, no, there's no need
to worry. Wadesdah was
alerted, and it's only thirty
miles away. They'll soon be
out looking for us.

A few minutes later . . .

I say, Captain, if we stay here they'll
take us back to Wadesdah, and we'll be
expelled once again . . . Wait a minute,
Snowy . . . It seems to be about thirty
miles to the city. Suppose we make
ourselves scarce . . .

On foot?

Wooah!
Wooah!

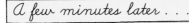

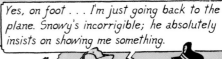

Yes, on foot . . . I'm just going back to the
plane. Snowy's incorrigible; he absolutely
insists on showing me something.

So you're
coming
at last!

All right, Snowy . . . I'm coming with you.

Thirty miles!
A mere trifle!

Thirty miles . . .
And I've still got
. . . Let's see . . .
I've still got . . .

. . . half a bottle of
whisky . . . that's
240 miles to the
gallon . . . not too
good, but still . . .

BOOM

My bottle! . . . I must save my bottle!

Thundering typhoons! The plane's blown up!

But my bottle's safe!

Columbus! . . . Tintin?

He went towards the plane . . . Let's hope . . . Careful: mustn't break my bottle . . .

TINTIN! . . . TINTIN! . . .

SMASH

Billions of blistering barnacles!

Tintin, old man! . . . You aren't broken? . . . I mean . . . you aren't hurt?

N . . . no. I was just knocked flat by the blast. But Snowy? Where's Snowy?

Safe and sound. He's fetching your hat.

Snowy, good old Snowy. You scented danger, eh? . . . And I just thought you wanted to play.

You know, Tintin, you ought to take me more seriously.

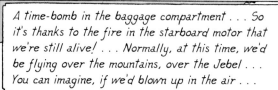

A time-bomb in the baggage compartment . . . So it's thanks to the fire in the starboard motor that we're still alive! . . . Normally, at this time, we'd be flying over the mountains, over the Jebel . . . You can imagine, if we'd blown up in the air . . .

Yes, we've had a lucky escape. I wonder . . .

What?

Nothing . . . but I think we won't hang around here. Let's go.

All right. I agree.

When we get to Wadesdah, we'll seek shelter with our old friend Senhor Oliveira de Figueira.

SNIFF SNIFF

We mustn't run into the rescue party on the way ... As soon as our disappearance is reported, they'll start searching for us.

WOOAAH ... YOW ... YEOW ...

Night has fallen ...

I've had enough of this little jaunt! ... If we go on much longer I'll be on my knees! If only I could lie down!

Lie down? We simply must reach Wadesdah before dawn, Captain. Lying down is out of the question.

Quick, lie down!

Make up your mind ... shall I lie down, or not?

A patrol! I'm sure they're out looking for us.

Halt! ... Who goes there?

I heard a noise ... a sort of rumbling ...

It's just an aeroplane ... Listen.

For heaven's sake stop snoring!

Me, snoring? I didn't hear anything.

Whew! ... They've gone.

Oh, good ... ZZZ ...

Come on, Captain, get up. We're moving on.

I'll have my breakfast in bed, Nestor ... ZZZ ... ZZZ ...

It isn't Nestor, Captain, it's Tintin! ... Get up, hurry!

ZZZ

What on earth can I do? Let's hope they don't come back ...

ZZZ ... ZZZ ... ZZZ ...

I always keep a small flask of rum for emergencies. Now's the time to use it . . .

This confounded cork won't come out . . .

Ah! . . . That's it!

POP

POP = ||| 🦷🦷 = 🍾 🦷🦷 = WHISKY

Stop! That's enough!

Aaah! Now then, where are those sprouts? . . . I mean scouts . . . ? I'd l-l-like a word or two w-w-with them!

Sh! Be quiet! We must get on.

Early next day . . .

Wadesdah at last! Now we must be careful . . . The main gates will be watched; but I know a small gateway, and that'll be unguarded.

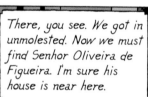

There, you see. We got in unmolested. Now we must find Senhor Oliveira de Figueira. I'm sure his house is near here.

Yes, that's it. I remember.

You did say he always has a bottle of wine handy?

Senhor Oliveira! . . . Senhor Oliveira! . . .

The joke's on us if he's moved!

Senhor Oliveira! . . . Senhor Oliveira! . . . Open the door! It's Tintin!

?

Blistering barnacles! . . . A patrol!

Quick, we must find somewhere to hide!

Who's that?

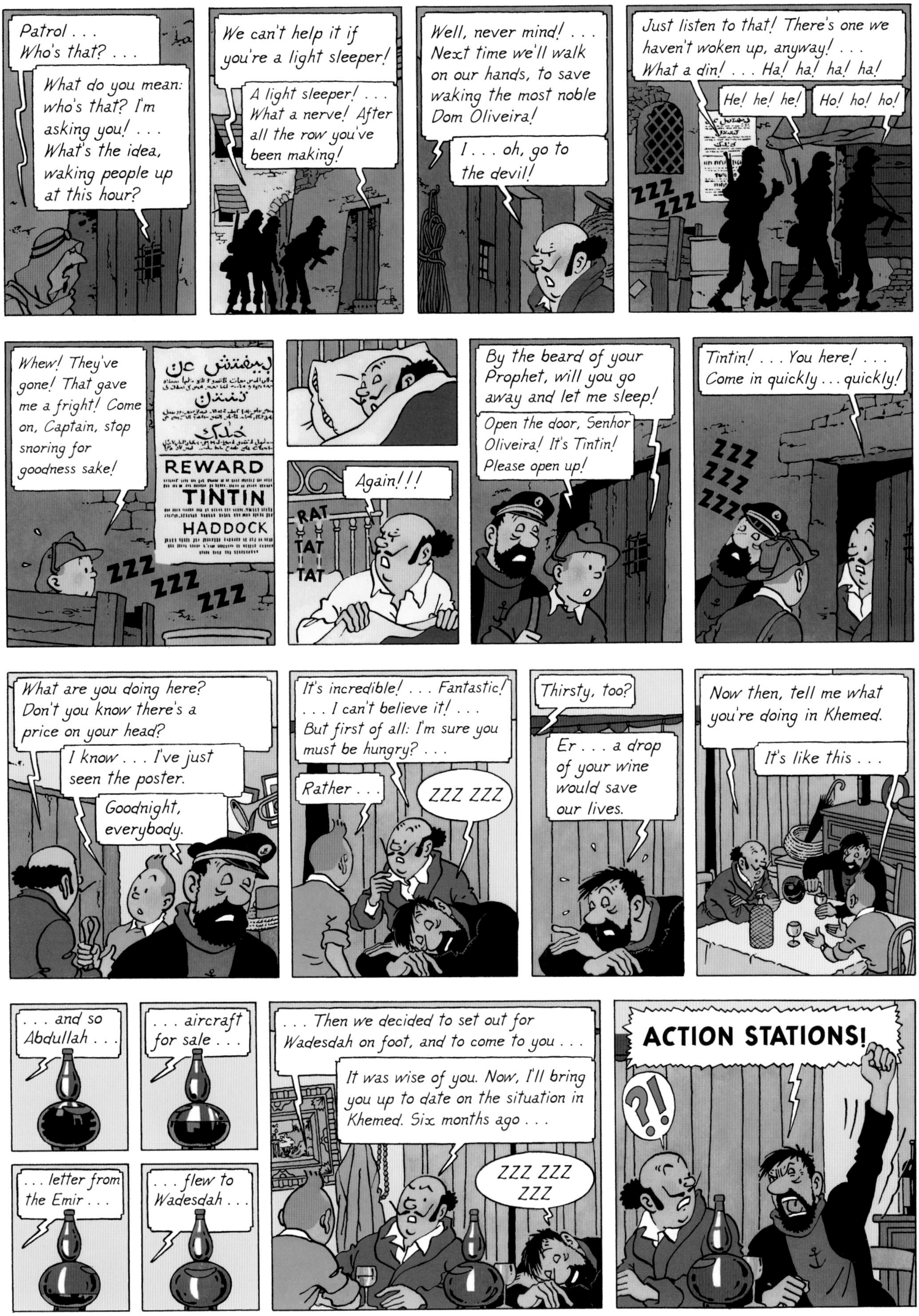
Patrol . . . Who's that? . . .
What do you mean: who's that? I'm asking you! . . . What's the idea, waking people up at this hour?
We can't help it if you're a light sleeper!
A light sleeper! . . . What a nerve! After all the row you've been making!
Well, never mind! . . . Next time we'll walk on our hands, to save waking the most noble Dom Oliveira!
I . . . oh, go to the devil!
Just listen to that! There's one we haven't woken up, anyway! . . . What a din! . . . Ha! ha! ha! ha!
He! he! he!
Ho! ho! ho!
ZZZ ZZZ
Whew! They've gone! That gave me a fright! Come on, Captain, stop snoring for goodness sake!
REWARD
TINTIN
HADDOCK
ZZZ ZZZ ZZZ
Again!!!
RAT TAT TAT
By the beard of your Prophet, will you go away and let me sleep!
Open the door, Senhor Oliveira! It's Tintin! Please open up!
Tintin! . . . You here! . . . Come in quickly . . . quickly!
ZZZ ZZZ ZZZ
What are you doing here? Don't you know there's a price on your head?
I know . . . I've just seen the poster.
Goodnight, everybody.
It's incredible! . . . Fantastic! . . . I can't believe it! . . . But first of all: I'm sure you must be hungry? . . .
Rather . . .
ZZZ ZZZ
Thirsty, too?
Er . . . a drop of your wine would save our lives.
Now then, tell me what you're doing in Khemed.
It's like this . . .
. . . and so Abdullah . . .
. . . aircraft for sale . . .
. . . letter from the Emir . . .
. . . flew to Wadesdah . . .
. . . Then we decided to set out for Wadesdah on foot, and to come to you . . .
It was wise of you. Now, I'll bring you up to date on the situation in Khemed. Six months ago . . .
ZZZ ZZZ ZZZ
ACTION STATIONS!
?!

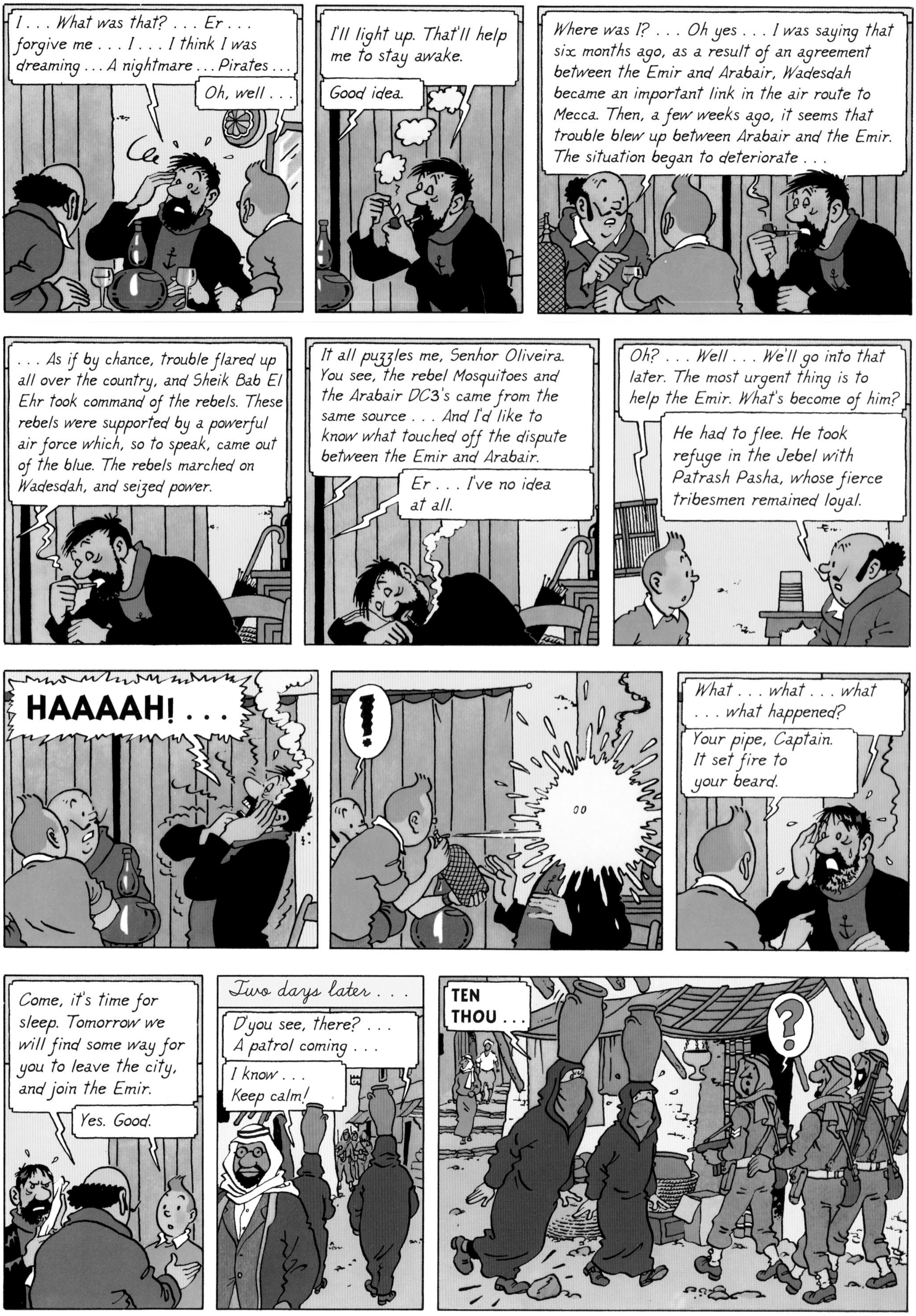

I . . . What was that? . . . Er . . . forgive me . . . I . . . I think I was dreaming . . . A nightmare . . . Pirates . . .
Oh, well . . .
I'll light up. That'll help me to stay awake.
Good idea.
Where was I? . . . Oh yes . . . I was saying that six months ago, as a result of an agreement between the Emir and Arabair, Wadesdah became an important link in the air route to Mecca. Then, a few weeks ago, it seems that trouble blew up between Arabair and the Emir. The situation began to deteriorate . . .
. . . As if by chance, trouble flared up all over the country, and Sheik Bab El Ehr took command of the rebels. These rebels were supported by a powerful air force which, so to speak, came out of the blue. The rebels marched on Wadesdah, and seized power.
It all puzzles me, Senhor Oliveira. You see, the rebel Mosquitoes and the Arabair DC3's came from the same source . . . And I'd like to know what touched off the dispute between the Emir and Arabair.
Er . . . I've no idea at all.
Oh? . . . Well . . . We'll go into that later. The most urgent thing is to help the Emir. What's become of him?
He had to flee. He took refuge in the Jebel with Patrash Pasha, whose fierce tribesmen remained loyal.
HAAAAH! . . .
What . . . what . . . what . . . what happened?
Your pipe, Captain. It set fire to your beard.
Come, it's time for sleep. Tomorrow we will find some way for you to leave the city, and join the Emir.
Yes. Good.
Two days later . . .
D'you see, there? . . . A patrol coming . . .
I know . . . Keep calm!
TEN THOU . . .

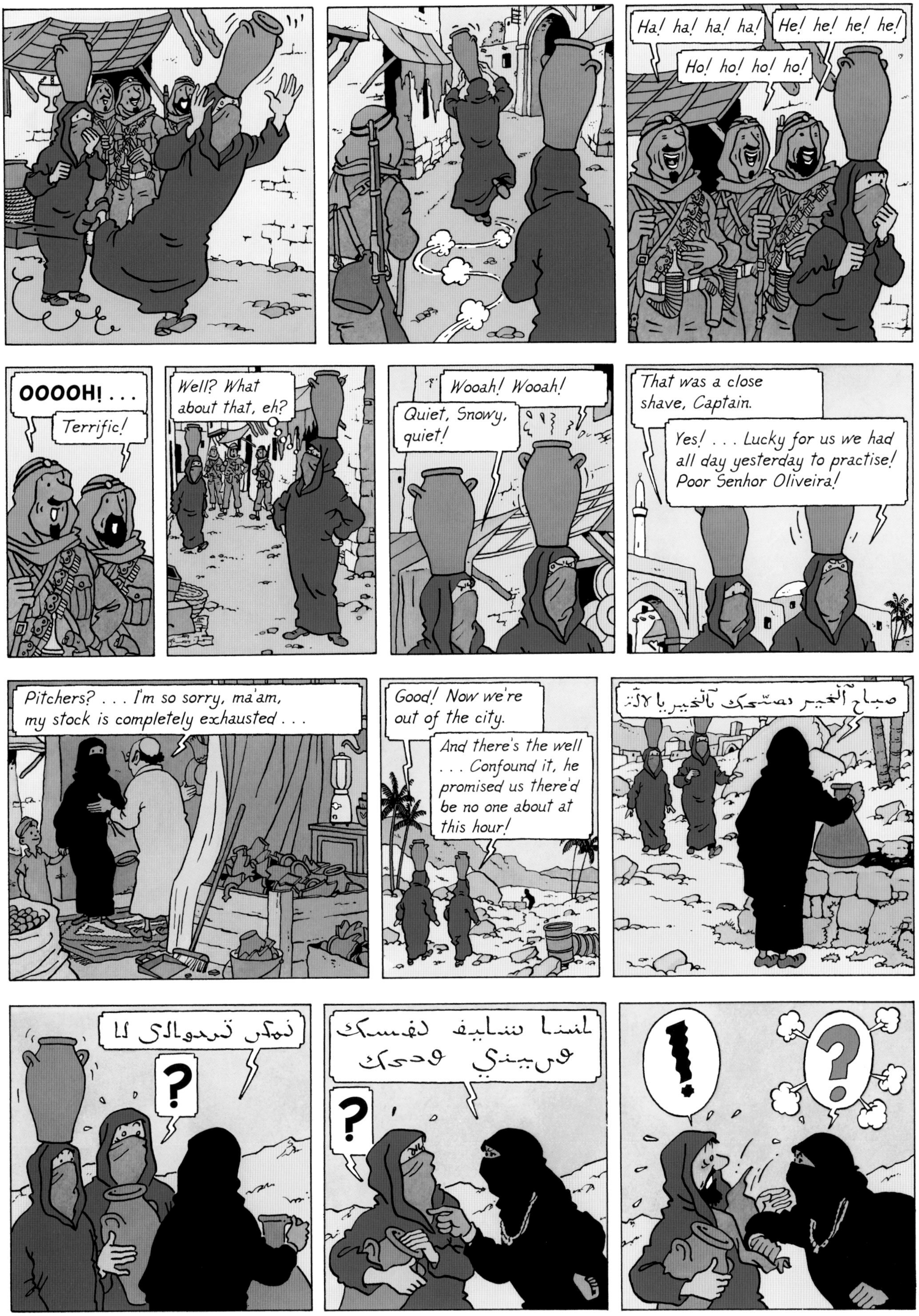
Ha! ha! ha! ha!
He! he! he! he!
Ho! ho! ho! ho!
OOOOH! . . .
Terrific!
Well? What about that, eh?
Wooah! Wooah!
Quiet, Snowy, quiet!
That was a close shave, Captain.
Yes! . . . Lucky for us we had all day yesterday to practise! Poor Senhor Oliveira!
Pitchers? . . . I'm so sorry, ma'am, my stock is completely exhausted . . .
Good! Now we're out of the city.
And there's the well . . . Confound it, he promised us there'd be no one about at this hour!
صباح الخير
?
?
!
?

Why can't you talk English like everyone else, you fancy-dress Fatima?! What do you want, anyway?

WOOAH!

Billions of blue blistering barnacles! That old witch will raise the alarm! . . .

. . . And our guide isn't here! . . . Oliveira was quite definite that he'd wait near the well, with the horses . . . Now what is it, Snowy?

Wooah! . . . Wooah! . . .

There he is! Fine! Back in the saddle again . . .

And a few minutes later . . .

My stirrups, blistering barnacles! . . . My stirrups! . . .

Meanwhile . . .

Hello, Colonel Achmed? . . . This is Mull Pasha at Sheik Bab El Ehr's headquarters . . . Order your Mosquitoes to take off immediately . . . Hello? . . . Yes. Their mission: to wipe out a party of three horsemen who have left Wadesdah, heading for the Jebel . . . You understand? . . . Good . . . Armoured cars are already on the way . . . Hello? . . . Yes, they are partisans of Ben Kalish Ezab . . . Yes, wipe them out.

There they are! . . . Fire!

Oh! . . . Listen! . . . Gunfire somewhere in the desert.

BOM
BOM
RAT TAT-TAT-TAT
RAT - TAT

Our own aircraft! They're mad!!

Hello! Black Panther calling. First mission accomplished; the two armoured cars in flames.

Hello, yes . . . Ah, mission accomplished . . . Excellent . . . The two armoured cars destroyed? . . . Congratulations, Colonel Achmed. Real aces, your pilots!

The armoured . . .
WHAT? . . .

Quick, put me back to Colonel Achmed . . . Ah, it's you . . . Er . . . I think I misunderstood. You didn't say that the armoured cars . . .

. . . were destroyed. . . . Yes, just as you ordered. I've already passed on your congratulations to the pilots . . . Pardon? . . .

What?? I ordered it??? . . . You bungling oaf! Only the horsemen were to be wiped out!

. . . Military tribunal . . . Court-martial . . . Dismissed . . . Reduced to the ranks . . .

Meanwhile . . .

I wouldn't be surprised if they're looking for us.

Whew! They've gone over. Into the saddle: we've a long way to go.

Next day, at dawn . . .

ZZZ . . . ZZZ

Careful! . . . Every man pick his target!

ZZZZ

HALT!

Friends! . . . Friends! . . . Don't shoot!

Friends? . . . We will soon see . . . Give the password!

The camels bark . . . er, no . . . The dogs bark and the camels pass.

Good . . . Come forward. Who are these strangers?

Friends of Ben Kalish Ezab. They have travelled far to see him.

That is good. We will take them before him.

These holes in the rock? . . . Yes, I noticed them. They look like windows. It wouldn't surprise me if there were people living inside.

Nonsense! They couldn't possibly. Still, we'll soon find out . . .

Living in there! That's a good one!

لحّ شي ذزيد لكعر شوتّنت دا،

Beg pardon, ma'am!

All right. People do live there . . .

I . . . Oh, look there!

(28)

Thundering typhoons! . . . A Roman temple, hewn from the rock! . . . Incredible!

We have arrived.

A few minutes later . . .

How stupendous! An entire city carved out of the mountain.

Tintin! . . . Captain! . . . You here? . . . It is unbelievable!

And my son? . . . My own little treasure? My precious darling . . . Where is he?

Ah, yes . . . We left him at Marlinspike, Your Highness. But rest assured, he is in good hands.

Poor little lamb! How sad he must be, so far from his Papa.

And now I'll leave you tied to the palm tree, so the crocodiles can come and eat you. Ha! ha! We're having fun, aren't we, Nestor? . . .

Confounded brat! . . . Ah, someone's coming. They'll set me free.

Ah, Nestor, I was looking for you. Could you give me a hand? It's nothing much: simply give me a little push.

Mmmm! . . . Mmm!

It's to test the new steering mechanism I've fitted to my roller-skates . . . Quite simple, really. They use the same principle for steering model cars.

Mmm! . . . Mm!

For instance, at the moment, my skates are locked right over to the left . . . If someone were to push me now I should turn round more or less on the same spot.

Mmm! . . . Mmm!

But I'm quite sure that despite his sadness my cherub is a little ray of sunshine, bringing life and gaiety into your old home.

Undoubtedly!

And you, what brings you here? . . . Come along in and sit down. You must be tired. And you'll certainly be hungry and thirsty. I will have some refreshments brought to you.

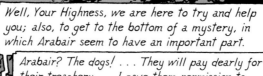

Well, Your Highness, we are here to try and help you; also, to get to the bottom of a mystery, in which Arabair seem to have an important part.

Arabair? The dogs! . . . They will pay dearly for their treachery . . . I gave them permission to establish a base at Wadesdah, an important link on the route to Mecca . . .

One day, about three months ago, my little Abdullah, my flawless jewel, expressed a wish to see the Arabair planes loop the loop a few times before landing at Wadesdah . . .

Loop the loop!? But, Highness . . .

Nothing simpler, don't you agree? . . . And it would have given my lambkin such pleasure! . . . Well, instead of seizing this opportunity of pleasing my little sugar-plum, they refused, on some trumped-up excuse . . .

But Highness . . .

Naturally, I was very angry and threatened to terminate our agreement. I also used another threat: that I would reveal to the world that Arabair are involved in slave trading.

WHAT? . . .

GRRR . . .

Slave trading, no less . . . Their planes touching down at Wadesdah on the way from Africa are always full to bursting with native Sudanese and Senegalese. These are Mohammedan converts, making their pilgrimage to Mecca.

Yes, go on . . .

On the other hand, on the return journey their planes are mostly empty . . . Why? . . . Because somewhere between Wadesdah and Mecca these unfortunate negroes are sold as slaves.

But that's frightful!

Er . . . Yes . . . But to get back to Arabair: these jackals stirred up trouble in my country, and thanks to their support, the accursed Bab El Ehr was able to seize power . . . But it won't be for long . . . I'll throw him out, that mangy dog, that stinking hyena, that slimy serpent, that . . .

GRAOW

By Allah! . . . Let us hope your dog hasn't gone near Ayesha!

GRRAOW **? !**

CRACK **GRAOW**

Achmed! . . . Quick! . . . Ayesha!

Hello! . . . You here too? . . .

Yes, a tame cheetah. But you see what happens when he is annoyed . . . And I am the same: woe betide those who attack me . . . The perfidious Bab El Ehr will learn this one day, to his cost!

GRRR! . . .

. . . And that infamous di Gorgonzola, too, the owner of Arabair.

Arabair belongs to di Gorgonzola?

It does indeed. Di Gorgonzola – shipping magnate, newspaper proprietor, radio, television and cinema tycoon, air-line king, dealer in pearls, gun-runner, trafficker in slaves – the man who helped Bab El Ehr to seize power . . . But patience! Ill-gotten gains benefit no one!

That's what he thinks!

He's an international crook; he must be put out of harm's way.

Yes, you are right. But what can we do to expose his dreadful traffic in slaves?

Tell me, Your Highness . . . Mecca is the terminus for Arabair, isn't it? . . . Good . . . Is there any way of actually getting us there?

Aha! . . . More and more interesting!

To Mecca? That's not easy at the moment. But if you will give me two or three days, I will find means of putting you aboard a sailing-ship, which will take you there.

Thank you, Highness.

Aha! This will please Bab El Ehr . . .

GRAOW!✳✱¡☆⊙

Again? What has happened now?

It is Ben Yussef, O Master . . . Ayesha jumped on him . . . See, it will be at least three weeks before he is well . . . It seems that he trod on Ayesha's tail . . .

Oh, poor creature!

Three days later . . .

There, everything is arranged. You leave tomorrow at dawn, with two trusted men. They will lead you to a point on the coast where a small vessel will be waiting to take you to Mecca. But be on your guard. Di Gorgonzola is a dangerous man.

Two days have passed . . .

Here we are . . . You may dismount . . . But stay while I make sure that the boat has arrived.

He's signalling to us . . . We can go.

Ah, so that's the tub we're going to board. It's a dhow . . . No; I beg your pardon: a sambuk.

Look, they have just put a boat out.

Danger! Danger! A mounted patrol!

By the beard of the Prophet, something suspicious is going on over there.

Halt! ... Who goes there?

By Allah! ... They have stumbled on a patrol! ...

BANG · BANG · BANG · BANG

BANG · BANG · BANG

Ha! ha! ha! Soldiers? Them? ... Don't make me laugh! One shot into the air and they bolted like rabbits!

At dawn ...

Ha! ha! ha! ha!

Ha! ha! ha! I was thinking of those twopenny-halfpenny coastguards galloping headlong! Anyone'd think they were trying to break the sound barrier!

Unfortunately they'll have made a report ... In which case ...

What a pessimist you are! What are you afraid of? ... That they'll send a squadron of battleships after us?

Not that, certainly, but ...

But what?

Over there, Captain! ... That's just what I feared!

Thundering typhoons! Mosquitoes!

They're coming back! ... This is going to be hot! ... Everybody down!

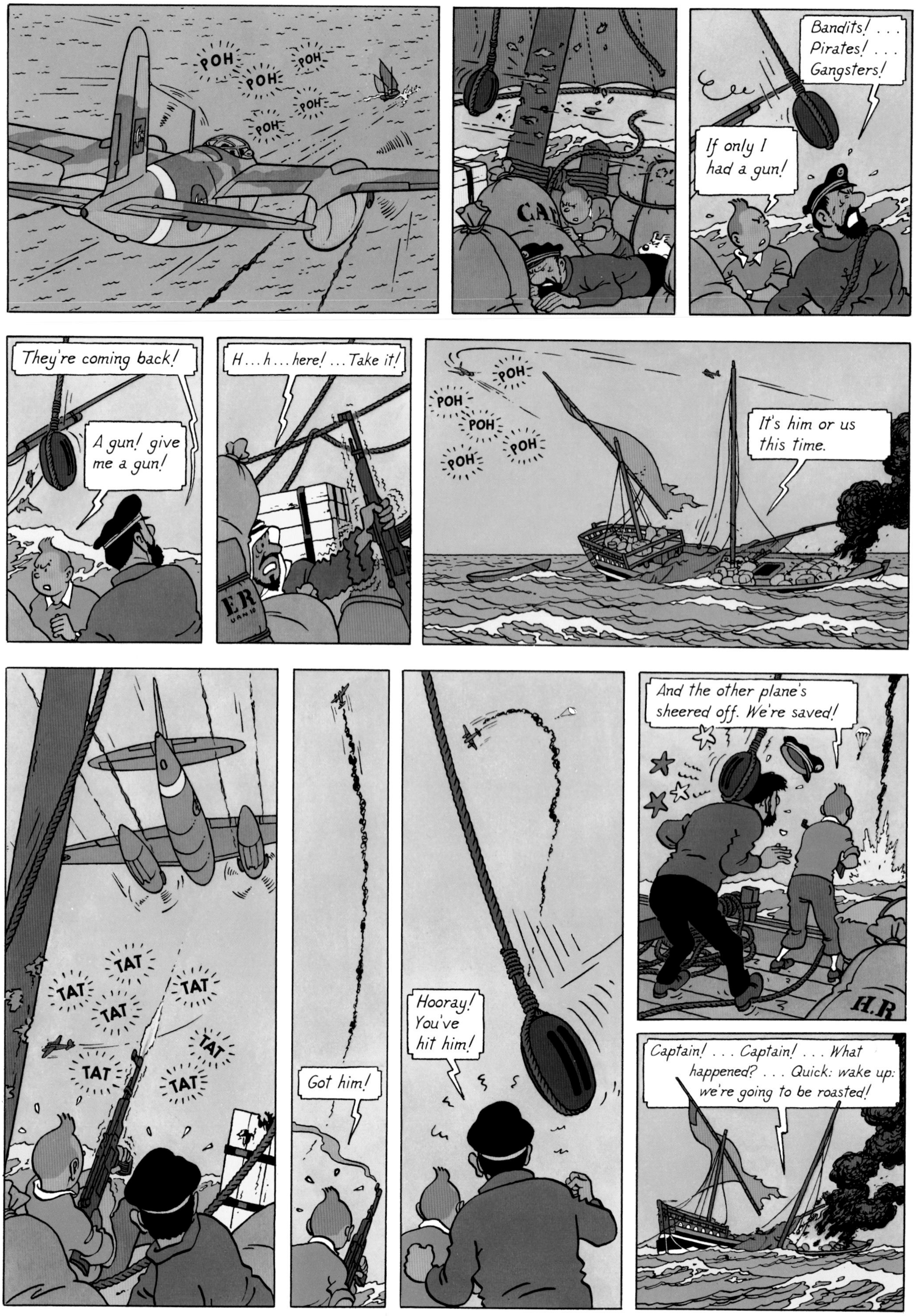

POH
POH
POH
POH
POH
Bandits! . . . Pirates! . . . Gangsters!
If only I had a gun!
They're coming back!
A gun! give me a gun!
H . . . h . . . here! . . . Take it!
POH
POH
POH
POH
POH
It's him or us this time.
TAT
TAT
TAT
TAT
TAT
TAT
TAT
Got him!
Hooray! You've hit him!
And the other plane's sheered off. We're saved!
Captain! . . . Captain! . . . What happened? . . . Quick: wake up: we're going to be roasted!

I don't know what happened . . . Some coward hit me from behind.

But who? . . . We're on our own. The crew have taken the boat and made off.

Quick, get down . . . That's what knocked you out!

Thundering typhoons! My nose!

So sorry . . . But there's no time to waste. We must build a raft, or we'll be grilled alive.

A quarter of an hour later . . .

Billions of blue blistering barnacles! . . . We've saved two cases of provisions, and no tin-opener; it's enough to drive you crazy!

What about trying with your knife?

Oh! There's the pilot from the plane we shot down!

Him!!! Let him take care of himself . . . Er . . . Is he far away?

No, quite near. Here, help me rescue him.

You've done a good job, eh? You trigger-happy thug! Who are you, anyway? What's your name?

Skut.

What do you mean, scoot? I'll teach you manners, you blithering bombardier. I'll soon deflate you! Ectoplasm!

But . . . but . . . my name Skut . . . Piotr Skut . . . Me Esthonian . . .

Look out! . . . Mind your knife!

BANG

Er . . . Oh! Skut . . . So your name's Skut, eh? . . . Er, I . . . Well, don't let it bother you!

Meanwhile . . .

Hello! hello! . . . This is R3KO . . . This is R3KO calling K6VM . . . Over.

Hello! Hello! This is K6VM . . . This is K6VM . . . Come in R3KO . . . Come in . . . Over.

35

Meanwhile . . .

May I have the pleasure of this samba, Princess?

But of course, Marquis.

What an ideal yacht for a cruise!

The "Scheherazade" is certainly a wonderful ship . . . And what a good idea to have a fancy-dress ball on board . . . Ma-a-arvellous!

Excuse me, my lord, there is a radio call for you . . . It's urgent . . .

Very well, I'm coming.

You see, dear lady? Business, always business. I am indeed a slave . . . Will you forgive me?

Don't give it a thought.

What an entrancing host he is. This cruise aboard the "Scheherazade" is really too enchanting!

Yes, he's a true gentleman. Naturally, malicious tongues spread rumours that he has a shady past . . .

It's only to be expected that such luxury arouses envy. One must admit . . .

Hello! Hello! K6VM calling R3KO . . . Transmit in code . . . Over.

Powerful insects have stung the blue goat. Parasites 1 and 2 are in the bag. Out.

K6VM to R3KO. Understood. Out.

Good . . . Now for the book, and we'll decode this. Parasites 1 and 2 – I know who they are!

There . . . I have it . . . Excellent! Mull Pasha has done well. We're rid of those two meddlers!

If this goes on, Captain, we'll soon be on Dr Bombard's diet: plankton and sea-water.

Me? . . . Drink sea-water? . . . Are you out of your mind?

Try some, Captain. It's not as bad as all that.

Ha! ha! ha! Not as bad as all that! . . . Think of all the dead fish there must be in it . . . All the people drowned in it over the centuries . . . All the tons of rubbish dumped from ships every day . . . You can commit suicide if you like, drinking that pig-swill. But for me it's "niet, niet", all along the line!

This not good . . .

Besides . . . Besides . . .

Besides . . . Besides . . .

YIPPEEE

?

There! . . . A ship! . . . Saved!

A ship . . . Just when you've swallowed that liquid manure! Ha! ha! ha! What a scream!

A ship! It's true!

Ha! ha! ha! This'll be the death of me!

Let's hope . . . let's hope they spot us!

!

SPLOSH

Who wasn't going to drink any sea-water? That'll teach him!

So you decided to have some after all!

Me? Not on your life! . . . Not a drop! . . . Glub!

Oh! The ship! She no see us! . . . She go! . . .

! ?

Thundering typhoons! He's right! . . . She's getting further away. Who's the bath-tub admiral commanding that crew of landlubbers?

What now? How can we attract their attention?

I've an idea! Has anyone got a mirror?

A mirror? What on earth for?

Here . . . I have one.

You like comb too?

Well done, Tintin! I never thought of it!

No thanks, only the mirror.

Blistering barnacles, go on! . . . Flash the sunlight straight in their eyes; they'll see us in the end.

Let's hope so! It's our last chance!

Flashing light to starboard, sir.

There, sir . . . Do you see it?

Yes, I see . . . A raft . . . with three men.

Hello? . . . Yes, Captain, go ahead . . . What? A raft with three shipwrecked sailors? By Lucifer . . . I . . . Wait, I'll come and see . . . Till then, not a word to my guests. I'm coming.

There, my lord . . . Do you see the signals they're making. Three of them, and a little dog.

By Lucifer! . . . Tintin and the bearded sailor . . . And a third ruffian! . . . But what about the message Mull Pasha just sent me?

Shall I alter course, sir?

A waste of time . . . They're just some more of those practical jokers who drift across the ocean in a nut-shell . . . You know, it's the three all the newspapers wrote about . . . They don't need anything. Proceed on your course.

But my lord Marquis . . .

I said proceed . . . Fire and brimstone! Where should we be if we stopped for all the rag-tag-and-bobtail who put out to sea for fun! . . . Proceed . . . And not a word of this to the passengers . . . You understand?

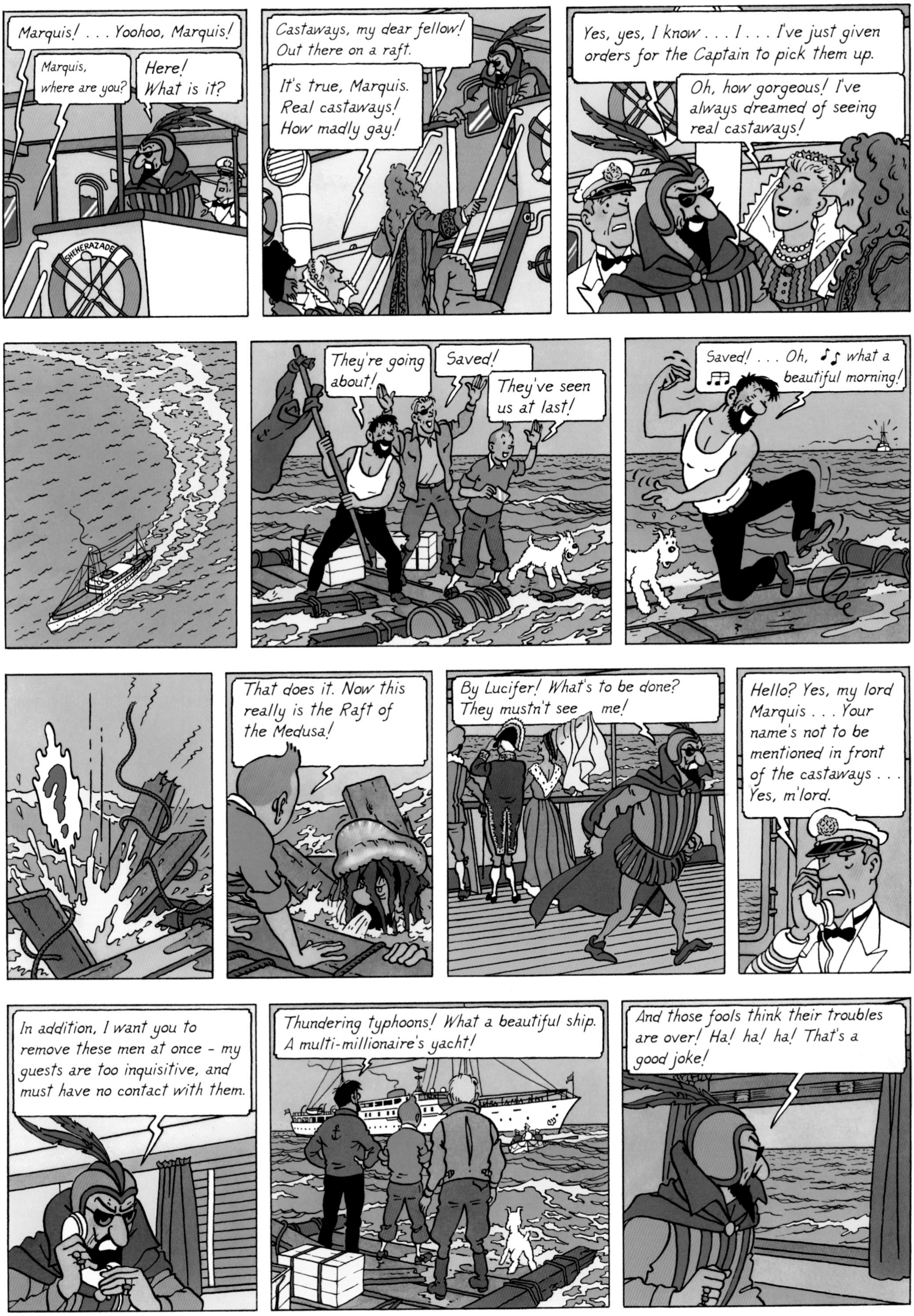

Marquis! . . . Yoohoo, Marquis!
Marquis, where are you?
Here! What is it?
Castaways, my dear fellow! Out there on a raft.
It's true, Marquis. Real castaways! How madly gay!
Yes, yes, I know . . . I . . . I've just given orders for the Captain to pick them up.
Oh, how gorgeous! I've always dreamed of seeing real castaways!
SHEHERAZADE
They're going about!
Saved!
They've seen us at last!
Saved! . . . Oh, what a beautiful morning!
That does it. Now this really is the Raft of the Medusa!
By Lucifer! What's to be done? They mustn't see me!
Hello? Yes, my lord Marquis . . . Your name's not to be mentioned in front of the castaways . . . Yes, m'lord.
In addition, I want you to remove these men at once - my guests are too inquisitive, and must have no contact with them.
Thundering typhoons! What a beautiful ship. A multi-millionaire's yacht!
And those fools think their troubles are over! Ha! ha! ha! That's a good joke!

Thundering typhoons! What a magnificent yacht! Whose is she? . . . Hey, are they having a carnival on board?

Almost . . . A fancy-dress ball . . . And what a bunch they are: high society, I can tell you; nothing but dukes, duchesses and film stars - all the nobs.

Per la Madonna! Can you believe it! . . . It's Tintin, and his friend the deep-sea fisherman, Paddock.

I must go and welcome them. Art must embrace the children of Adventure!

In the name of the Marquis di Gorgonzola welcome aboard, carissime mie!

Signora Castafiore! . . . Run for it! What shall we do? . . . Hop back on the raft?

My dear Tintin!

Delighted to see you again, my dear Padlock . . . er . . . Harrock.

. . . 'n roll, Signora Castoroili, Harrock'n-roll!

I'm so sorry, Signora, but his lordship has given orders: these poor men are completely exhausted. And then . . . there's the risk of infection, you know.

But my good man, I'm not ill!

A little later . . .

Well, Parker, have you questioned them?

Yes, m'lord. They were aboard a sambuk, being taken to Mecca . . .

. . . This morning, their boat was machine-gunned and set on fire by aircraft from Khemed. After shooting down one of the planes, they made themselves a raft. They then rescued the pilot of the aircraft.

Well done, Parker. Thank you.

If your lordship will pardon me, I think I should mention that Signora Castafiore, who knows the two castaways, welcomed them in your lordship's name.

Diavolo!

The Marquis di Gorgonzola's yacht! . . . It's fantastic . . . I must be dreaming.

Come on, Tintin . . . Up in the clouds again? . . . Hey! Tintin!

They can't stay here on board. But what's to be done? What indeed? . . . Ah, I have it! The "Ramona". . . . She's in these waters . . . Tomorrow we must pass one another, as if by chance.

Get dressed quickly. You're in luck. We've met a merchantman bound for Mecca: just where you were making for. Her master has agreed to take you aboard.

Er . . . I . . . What . . . Good, that's fine.

RAMONA
PANAMA RP

So that's that! And now, my fine friends, I wish you a pleasant journey. Ha! ha! ha! ha!

Ah, this is the place for me: back aboard a good old freighter.

There, you two: these are your quarters. Your pal's going elsewhere . . . The skipper will be down to see you soon: he'll bring you your whisky himself!

Hi, you lubberly scum, not so fast! What do you mean?

This is too much! He's locked us in, the insolent porcupine!

Open up! Thundering typhoons, open up! You ill-mannered savages!

THUMP
THUMP

Well, well, you old drunkard! So you're kicking up a row already?

Allan!!

!

This is a happy reunion, eh, old bottle-nose? We must have a drink on it.

Allan! What's going on? How have we . . .

. . . ended up here? Quite simple: I command one of di Gorgonzola's freighters. Yesterday I had a signal ordering me to alter course. So this morning we met the "Scheherazade", as if by accident . . . Neatly done, eh?

Very! And may we inquire what you plan to do with us?

If you're sensible, you'll be put ashore. But not at Mecca . . . At Wadesdah!

Wadesdah! But that's murder! Sheik Bab El Ehr has put a price on our heads . . .

You're breaking my heart, dear boy. But that's enough talk . . . You must be thirsty . . . Here, drink my health . . .

Not on your life! . . . And you'll put us ashore at Mecca, or else!

Or else what? . . . Ha! ha! ha! . . . I advise you to behave yourselves. Don't forget we're in the Red Sea, and there's no shortage of sharks . . . You get me? . . . Now, like a big-hearted chap, I'll leave this bottle to console you.

'Bye for now! . . . We dock the day after tomorrow. So you've plenty of time to solve one important question: do you sleep with your beard under or over the sheet?

Ha! ha! ha! . . . That's a good one! His beard!

Yes, he won't sleep a wink tonight!

Over? . . . No, not that way . . .

Under? . . . Blistering barnacles! Not that way either!

Stay! . . . Once a drunkard . . .

. . . always a drunkard!

Go on! Just a little sip . . .

Well, why not?

CRASH

Over? . . .

Under? . . .

To Beelzebub with the bedclothes! I'm too hot anyway!

There . . . That's the answer!

Now for some sleep . . . at last.

BANG THUMP ✦ THIS WAY! HURRY! BANG CLOMP INTO THE BOATS!

There, I'm dreaming already!

COME ON, JOE! ✦ BANG

Hey, this is no dream! . . . Those shouts . . . that stampeding . . . The engines have stopped . . . that's real enough!

Show a leg, there!

?

Did . . . did you fall out of your bunk?

Where d'you think I came from? . . . Mars? . . . Blistering barnacles, get up! . . . I think that bunch of rats are abandoning ship!

Open up, thundering typhoons! . . . Open up before I get violent!

Captain, this sea-chest. Let's try to force the door.

BUMP BUMP BUMP

Quick, let's see what's happening.

YEOW!

C. OLSSON

Hurry, Captain, hurry!

Thundering typhoons! The ship's on fire!

Keep it up, boys! Row hard! She'll blow up any minute.

43

Wreckers! ... Pirates! ...
Filibusters! ... Picaroons!
Leaving us in the lurch on a
doomed ship! To Davy Jones
with the lot of you!

Follow me ... We'll probably
find a raft up for'ard.

We obviously have
a vocation for
shipwrecks!

HEY!
HELP! HELP!

EFFENDI!
EFFENDI!

There's someone
in the hold! ...
What the ... ?!

Who are you, below there?

We good black
men ... Want come
out ... No can
breathe ... We
afraid ...

Negroes! A lot of
them, too, I'd say ...
What shall we do,
Captain? We can't
just abandon them.

You're right.
Come on.

We'll try and put out the
blaze ... That cargo ...
I just can't make it out!

Eighteen tons of high explosive
and ammunition: it'll make a pretty
fireworks display!

That's it! The hose is
connected ... Now then,
let's open the valve.

Blub ... I ... blub
... I've got it,
Cap ... blub ...

Thanks ... that's it ... I'll tackle
the fire ... You go over to port
and get another hose into action.

Let's hope this will do the job!

What about the explosion? Is it due for today or . . . But . . . but . . . I can't see any more smoke or flames!

By thunder! The fire's gone out! Put her about boys. We're going back.

It . . . it's out . . . A huge wave . . . I was very nearly washed overboard . . .

What luck! . . . Now for those poor fellows below, Captain.

You're right, but first of all . . .

. . . I'm going to try to restart the engines. You go up on the bridge and take the wheel.

Half an hour later . . .

By thunder! . . . The "Ramona" is drawing away! . . . Someone has got her engines going!

Phew! that was no joke, alone; but she's under way at last.

Magnificent, Captain . . . And now for the Negroes.

There's something more urgent: to send out a distress call by radio.

! OH!

Look! Skut! . . . Dead?

No, he's alive . . . See, he's coming round.

Skut! Skut, old man, say something! What happened?

You escape! Hurry! . . . Hurry! . . . The fire! . . . Ship full of ammunition! . . . Hurry before explosion . . .

Ammunition! The pirates! . . . That's why they deserted like rats . . .

Don't worry, Skut: the fire's out. There's no more danger . . . But what about you? What happened?

They wake me, to go with them . . . Without you . . . I refuse . . . I want to . . . er . . . wake you . . . and send radio signal.

Then they are angry . . . Break radio and fight with me . . . Then I . . . knocked-out. They go?

Yes, they abandoned us, the iconoclasts. So here we are alone on board, with a crowd of Negroes in the hold.

You like . . . I can help you . . . Repair radio, perhaps, send S.O.S. . . .

Good idea . . . Do that . . . I'm going to make sure there's no further danger.

A little later . . .

No more need to worry, youngster: the fire is right out.

Now I'll take care of those Negroes. First, to let them out . . .

Save poor Muslim!

Me ill. Me dying.

All right! I'm coming now!

Hey there! . . . Let go of me!! . . . HELP, TINTIN! . . . HELP!

Troglodytes! . . . Sea-gherkins! . . . Pickled herrings! Leave me alone!

Back, visigoths! . . . Back, anacoluthons!

Hang on, Captain! . . . I'm coming! . . .

All right! I'm here!

So sorry, Captain, but I had no choice.

Please don't worry: I'm getting used to it!

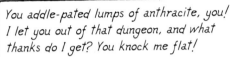

You addle-pated lumps of anthracite, you! I let you out of that dungeon, and what thanks do I get? You knock me flat!

Effendi not be angry . . . You not shout . . . We not know you good white man . . . We think you bad white man who shut poor black man in bottom of ship . . . Where are bad white men?

Bad white men all gone. Left us. But if you help me, I'll take you wherever you want to go. You're going to Mecca, eh?

Yes, Effendi, to Mecca. We good Muslims. We making pilgrimage to the tomb of the Prophet.

All right, we'll take you to Mecca . . . on condition that you all obey my orders. For a start, I need some men as stokers.

Me, Effendi . . .

Me . . .

Me . . .

Me, Effendi . . .

Two days later . . .

There. If my reckoning is correct we should soon sight Jidda, the port for Mecca.

Yes. Those poor fellows . . . nearly the end of their journey.

Poor fellows! . . . Poor fellows! . . . You don't still believe they were being sold as slaves? . . . It's absurd . . .

If the Emir was telling the truth, then I'm afraid that was to be their fate.

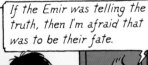

Come, come, you've been reading too many thrillers . . . There's no slave-trading nowadays!

Look, Captain; just tell me this: is there any coke aboard?

Any . . . any coke? . . . But . . .

Effendi! Effendi! You come look! . . . Ship coming to us . . .

!

47

So it is! A sambuk . . . The harbour pilot from Jidda, perhaps . . . No, we're still too far from shore . . . A fisherman, then?

How odd . . . he's signalling to us . . . We'll heave to, and see what he wants . . .

Salaams, O sailor . . . Captain Allan is up there?

Captain Allan? . . . Finished . . . Gone . . . I am captain now.

Ah, you have replaced him . . . Good, good . . . Is the coke of best quality this time?

The coke?? Again? Blistering barnacles, what's all this nonsense about coke? Thundering typhoons, there's no coke on board!

No coke on board! . . . Ha! ha! ha!

Hmm . . . Yes . . . Strong muscles . . . You'll do . . .

And teeth? . . . Come on, open your mouth, Sambo . . . Hmm, not too bad . . . Teeth quite sound . . .

Come here, you.

Yes, Effendi.

Here, have you quite finished playing the cattle-dealer? This man's not a horse, nor a slave . . .

Ssh! . . . You mustn't say that! . . . "Coke" is the word, as you well know.

Coke!! . . . Blistering barnacles! . . . Tintin was right! There still are slave-traders . . . And that's what you're up to, you brute!

You trafficker in human flesh! You deserve to be strung up on the mizzen yardarm!

LOOK OUT!

ZZINNG

You cut-throat, you! . . . You're lucky I don't stuff your beard down your gullet! . . . But get out . . . viper! And take care that you don't cross my path again!

Sheer off, filibuster! . . . Out of my sight, you gallows bird!

Baboon! . . . Carpet-seller! . . . Paranoiac! . . . Pockmark! . . . Cannibal!

Duck-billed platypus! . . . Jellied-eel! . . . Bashi-bazouk! . . . Anthropophagus! . . . Cercopithecus! . . . Psychopath! . . . Er . . .

No good, Captain. He's too far away now . . .

That's what you think! He hasn't heard the last of me!

Where now?

On to the bridge.

PIRATE! ECTOPLASM COELACANTH VULTURE!

BODY-SNATCHER! OSTROGOTH! VANDAL!

This time . . . I think he really is out of earshot.

Yes! . . . More's the pity . . . dirty slave-trader!

By the way . . . How did you tumble to the word "coke"?

I'll show you.

I found this scrap of paper on the table while you were plotting our course on the chart. Read it.

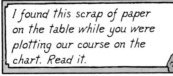

di Gorgonzola to Captain Ramona
Deliver Coke to the el Kaid at Jidda

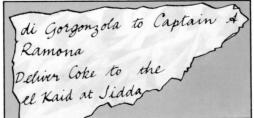

By the beard of the Prophet, the dog will pay dearly for this!

A fragment of a wireless message sent by di Gorgonzola to that gangster Allan! . . . And "coke" is a code word for their cargo of slaves! . . . The pirates!

First, we must talk to the Africans: they must be made to understand that under the circumstances it's madness for them to go to Mecca.

Agreed . . . Then we must try to send out a radio call . . .

Getting on, Skut?

Still much work, Captain.

Good . . . Well, I'm going to talk to the cargo. You take the wheel and steer due south. We'll head for Djibouti.

OK

A few minutes later . . .

My friends, listen to me carefully. You have undertaken this long journey to make a pilgrimage to Mecca, haven't you?

Yes.

Yes.

Afterwards, of course, you plan to return home and rejoin your families. Isn't that so?

Yes, Effendi.

Yes.

Yes.

I'm afraid a very different fate awaits you. You saw that Arab who came aboard, and I chased off? . . . He's waiting for you in Mecca, to buy you and make you into slaves! . . . Slaves, you understand?

You speak well, Effendi. Wicked Arab, very wicked. Poor black men not want to be slaves. Poor black men want to go to Mecca.

Naturally, I realise that. But I repeat, if you go there, you'll be sold as slaves. Is that what you want?

We not slaves, Effendi. We good Muslims. We want to go to Mecca.

But billions of blue blistering barnacles, I keep on telling you: if you go there, you'll be sold as slaves! Thundering typhoons, I can't make it any clearer.

You not shout, Effendi. Poor black men only want to go to Mecca.

All right, you boneheads, go to Mecca! . . . But you'll stay there for ever! . . . You'll never see your own country again! . . . Never see your families again! . . . You'll be slaves for ever! . . . That's what you're in for, you dunderheaded coconuts, you!

We not coconuts, Effendi. We good black men. We good Muslims. We want to go to Mecca.

I can't do a thing! . . . I've tried the lot! . . . You can't shift them: they want to go to Mecca, stop: that's all! . . . It's like banging your head against a brick wall!

Emyny sofoyi ooiboo-yi konychéeré!

Yirō!

Beyni!

Loyotō!

?

Now then . . . What's going on? . . . Why all the quarrelling?

I not want to go to Mecca. I tell them you are good white man, you speak truth. I remember in my village three young men went to Mecca . . . Two years ago . . . They not come back . . . They no doubt slaves . . . I not want to go to Mecca! . . . I not want to be slave.

Me too, I not go.

Me too!

Good, so I haven't preached in vain! . . . All right, we'll make a bargain: those who don't want to go to Mecca will be landed at another port. As for the rest, they can continue the voyage if they want to . . .

Good, Effendi.

The next morning . . .

There . . . the day after tomorrow we'll be at Djibouti, and that'll be the end of our worries . . .

Yes, if all goes well! I shan't be really happy till we get there. You can bet that at this very moment di Gorgonzola is aware of the situation. And he knows that we know . . . Watch out for what he's cooking up! . . .

BRRRRR

?

!

An aeroplane . . . They're circling us . . . how odd . . .

Hello, hello . . . Albatross to Shark . . . Have sighted Ramona 20 miles west of the Farasan Islands . . . She is steering south-south-east. Over.

Hello, hello . . . Shark to Albatross . . . Message received . . . Steering west . . .

. . . to intercept her . . . Out.

Aha! My orders have been carried out.

He's going off . . . I wonder what he was up to.

I don't know, but I don't much care for that sort of visit.

The trap is closing: my boys are on the job! . . . In a few hours the "Ramona" will have disappeared, with crew and cargo . . . So all the incriminating evidence will be effectively liquidated.

That plane snooping around worries me . . . If I were you, Captain, I'd alter course.

You're right . . . I'll do so.

A few hours later . . .

Well, Skut, how's the radio? Working?

No . . .

No! . . . The radio not working . . . I not find the trouble . . . I not know what more to do . . .

BRRRR

Again? . . .

The same one? . . .

Be careful, the wire!

OH!

?

The radio! Quite all broken now!

!

?

Hello . . . Albatross to Shark . . . Have found Ramona again.

Steering due south; she is 30 miles east of Dahlak-kebir Island.

That bird of ill-omen is getting on my nerves.

Buzz off, you stool-pigeon! You're asking for a smack on the nose!

Shark to Albatross. Ramona in sight. Preparing to dive.

I say, Skut, I'm terribly sorry! You've worked for so long on the radio . . . and then I'm so clumsy . . . Ssh!

She working! . . . She working now!

What?! . . . After a bang like that? It's not possible.

She working, I tell you! Listen . . .

!

BEEP-BEEP-BEEP

Captain! . . . Captain! . . . The radio! . . . It's going!!

I . . . So sorry, but the radio, Captain . . . The radio . . . It's going!!

Oh yes? Where? . . . I hope it steers clear of me . . .

. . . because I've had enough of being rammed! Only a couple of minutes ago, plop – a flying-fish slap in my face. And now you: that's enough!

Flying fish? I must have a look at them with my binoculars.

Oh, how beautiful! You'd think they were little silver arrows . . .

Look at them, skimming over the waves . . . I can see two . . . no, three . . .

And there . . . Hey, what in the world's that?

CAPTAIN! . . . CAPTAIN! . . . A PERISCOPE!

Where is it now? . . . I can't see it any more . . . But I'm absolutely sure . . .

Now then, keep calm . . .

There, Captain, over there, I'm sure . . . Right out there . . . I saw the wake, I tell you . . .

Now keep calm, young shaver! Periscope or no periscope, keep calm . . .

Ten thousand thundering typhoons! A periscope! . . . There! . . . It's true! . . .

Action stations! . . . Fire! . . . S.O.S. . . . The rudio, Skat! Confound! the radio, Skut! . . . Send for help! At once! . . . A submarine! . . . Clear the decks for action! . . . Keep calm! Don't panic! . . . Women and children first!

Calm down, Captain, calm down! . . . All isn't lost yet!

You're right . . . Keep cool . . . keep calm and don't panic!

Disaster! . . . The end! . . . There's nothing we can do! If they're di Gorgonzola's people we're finished!

But why?

The ammunition! . . . In the forward hold . . . A torpedo in there, and you know the rest!

Of course! Only the torpedo isn't here yet! Come on, hurry; everyone on the alert.

Not far away . . .

We're almost within range . . . They don't know what's in store for them.

This won't take long to settle . . . Stand by No. 1 tube . . .

Tintin at the radio. You at the wheel, Skut. Repeat my orders when I give them. Remember, starboard is right; port on the left . . .

S.O.S. . . . S.O.S. . . . s.s. Ramona calling. Unidentified submarine in immediate vicinity. . . . We fear the worst . . . Here is our   position.

No. 1 tube, fire!

S.O.S. . . . S.O.S. . . . s.s. Ramona calling . . . In danger of being torpedoed . . .

Torpedo to port! Hard a starboard! . . .

Hard a starboard it is!

Curses on them! They've swung away . . . They must have spotted us.

S.O.S. . . . S.O.S. . . . A torpedo has just missed us . . . S.O.S. . . . Hurry please . . . S.O.S.

A moment later, aboard the U.S.S. Los Angeles . . .

An S.O.S. I just picked up, sir.

What's all this ballyhoo about a submarine? . . . There isn't a war on, is there?

But meanwhile . . .

Starboard 20 . . . Ahead, speed six knots . . . Stand by No. 2 tube.

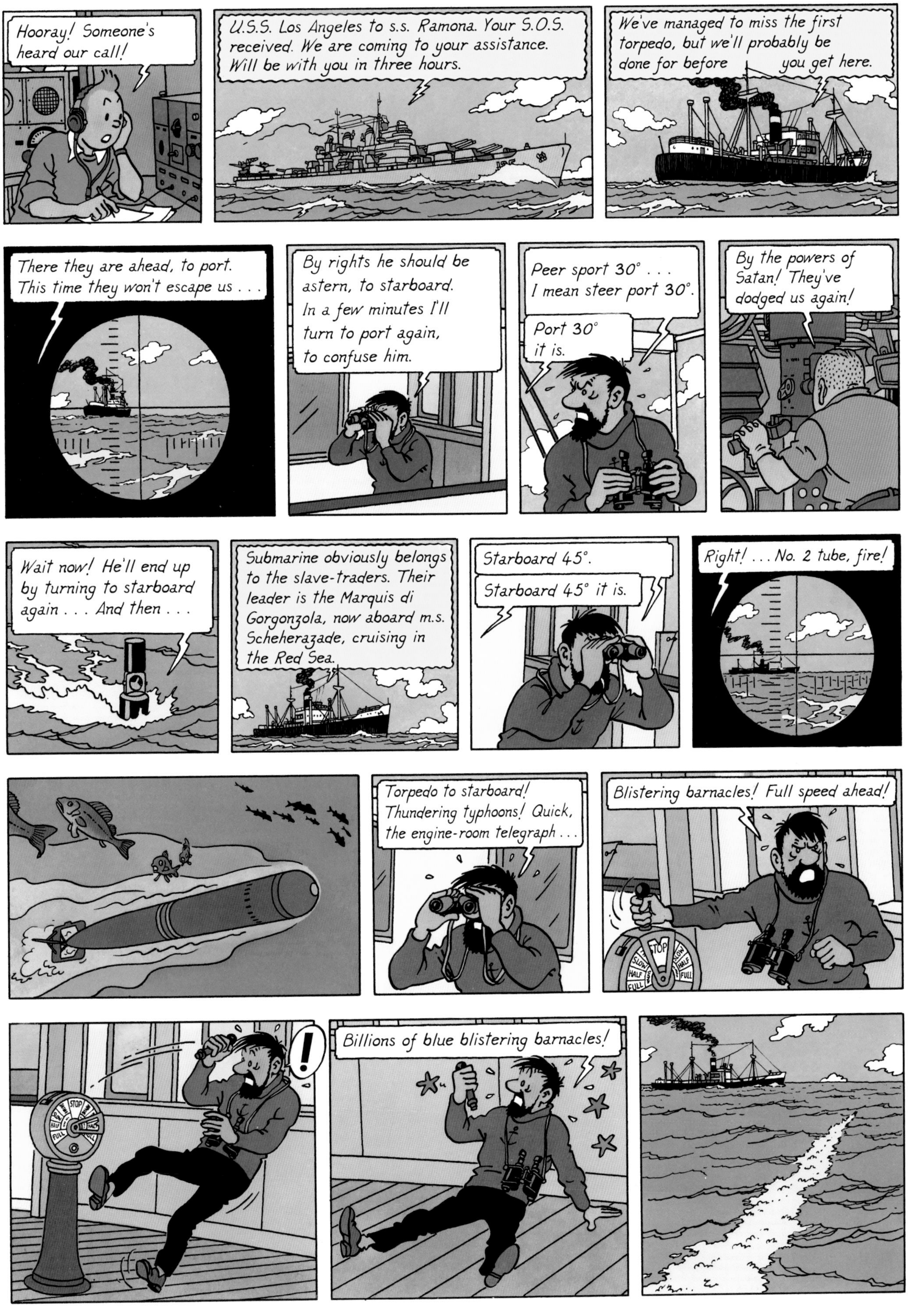

Hooray! Someone's heard our call!
U.S.S. Los Angeles to s.s. Ramona. Your S.O.S. received. We are coming to your assistance. Will be with you in three hours.
We've managed to miss the first torpedo, but we'll probably be done for before you get here.
There they are ahead, to port. This time they won't escape us . . .
By rights he should be astern, to starboard. In a few minutes I'll turn to port again, to confuse him.
Peer sport 30° . . . I mean steer port 30°.
Port 30° it is.
By the powers of Satan! They've dodged us again!
Wait now! He'll end up by turning to starboard again . . . And then . . .
Submarine obviously belongs to the slave-traders. Their leader is the Marquis di Gorgonzola, now aboard m.s. Scheherazade, cruising in the Red Sea.
Starboard 45°.
Starboard 45° it is.
Right! . . . No. 2 tube, fire!
Torpedo to starboard! Thundering typhoons! Quick, the engine-room telegraph . . .
Blistering barnacles! Full speed ahead!
!
Billions of blue blistering barnacles!

Thundering typhoons! The engine-room telegraph is jammed at half-speed astern. Quick, a screw-driver!

By Lucifer! They're going astern . . . our torpedo has missed again . . . They're tough, those boys . . .

Hooray! It's passed ahead of us.

S.O.S. A second torpedo has just missed. Hurry, Los Angeles.

Quick! Quick! I must release this infernal machine!

PCHKRAAPRVT! . . . TRRKHKRAA! . . . You confounded rattletrap . . .

. . . tin-can contraption! . . . Take that!

YEEOWW!

Ah, they're still going astern! Very well! No. 3 and No. 4 tubes ready?

CLING CLANG

Take that, you slot-machine, you!

?

Hello? . . . Engine room? . . . Hello?

Hello, Effendi?

BRROM

Too late! . . . They've got us!

56

BRROM!

Again!

No, they're depth charges! . . . Whew! I really thought we'd been torpedoed . . .

U.S. Navy seaplanes, with those pirates for a target! . . . They're certainly machines from the Los Angeles.

Oho! Great grandfathers! What a pasting! . . . They'll be as flat as a Dover sole after that!

Wait! . . . There, that upheaval in the water . . .

Look! The submarine has surfaced!

Yes . . . Obviously they've been badly knocked about . . .

Victory! . . . They're waving a white flag . . . They're surrendering . . . The game's up.

Hello, hello. Unidentified submarine: remain on the surface and stop your engines. One suspicious move and we'll blow you out of the water . . .

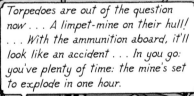

Torpedoes are out of the question now . . . A limpet-mine on their hull! . . . With the ammunition aboard, it'll look like an accident . . . In you go: you've plenty of time: the mine's set to explode in one hour.

Be quick: they're coming back!

Go!

What a job!

Saved! Yippee! Saved!

Hooray!

Tralalala-laika!

That is white man's folk-dance.

They said the ammunition was in the forepart . . .

Meanwhile . . .

This is all very fine, but we must wait for the Los Angeles. I'm going to see if there's any chance of dropping anchor.

Twenty-two fathoms depth . . . that's perfect . . .

Ahoy, there! Let go the anchor! Eighty fathoms of chain.

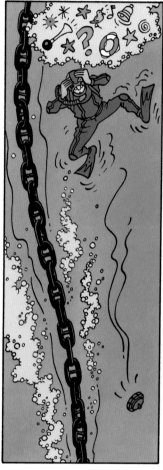

GLOOP

HIC   HIC

HIC

HIC   HIC

An hour later . . .

Hooray! . . . There she is! . . . The Los Angeles!

American cruiser in sight!

Don't worry, boys . . . She'll blow up any moment now.

HIC
BOOOM

? ? ? ? ?

The next morning . . .

Still no news from Kurt and his submarine . . . What are they playing at, the fools?

. . . and naval craft to intercept the m.s. Scheherazade and arrest the owner, name of Rastapopoulos, alias the Marquis di Gorgonzola . . .

Lost . . . all is lost! . . . But it's impossible!

RRING
RRING

Hello? . . . Yes . . . Come up on the bridge? . . . I haven't time, Captain. I . . . What? . . . A warship? . . . I . . . I'm coming now.

The cruiser Los Angeles, my lord Marquis . . . She's just flashed a signal ordering us to heave to. What shall I do?

Repeat the message, Tom . . . And add that if they don't heave to immediately, we'll open fire.

All right. Stop the engines. And launch my personal barge. I'll go myself and tell those insolent cowboys what I think of their manners! . . .

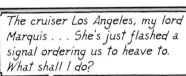

Ah, they've obeyed . . . Excellent! . . . But what are they doing now? . . .

It looks as if . . . yes, they're hoisting out a launch . . . and Rastapopoulos is going aboard . . .

Do not insist, my friends. I will go alone.

SHEHERAZADE

. . . And he's steering towards us! . . . Well, this beats everything! . . . To have the cheek to come and brazen it out! What a nerve!

But what's happening now? . . . He's slowing up. He's stopping . . . Has he broken down?

Great snakes! . . . He's sinking! . .

Whoops! That's done the trick! . . . Just you catch me now gentlemen! . . . Ha! ha! ha!

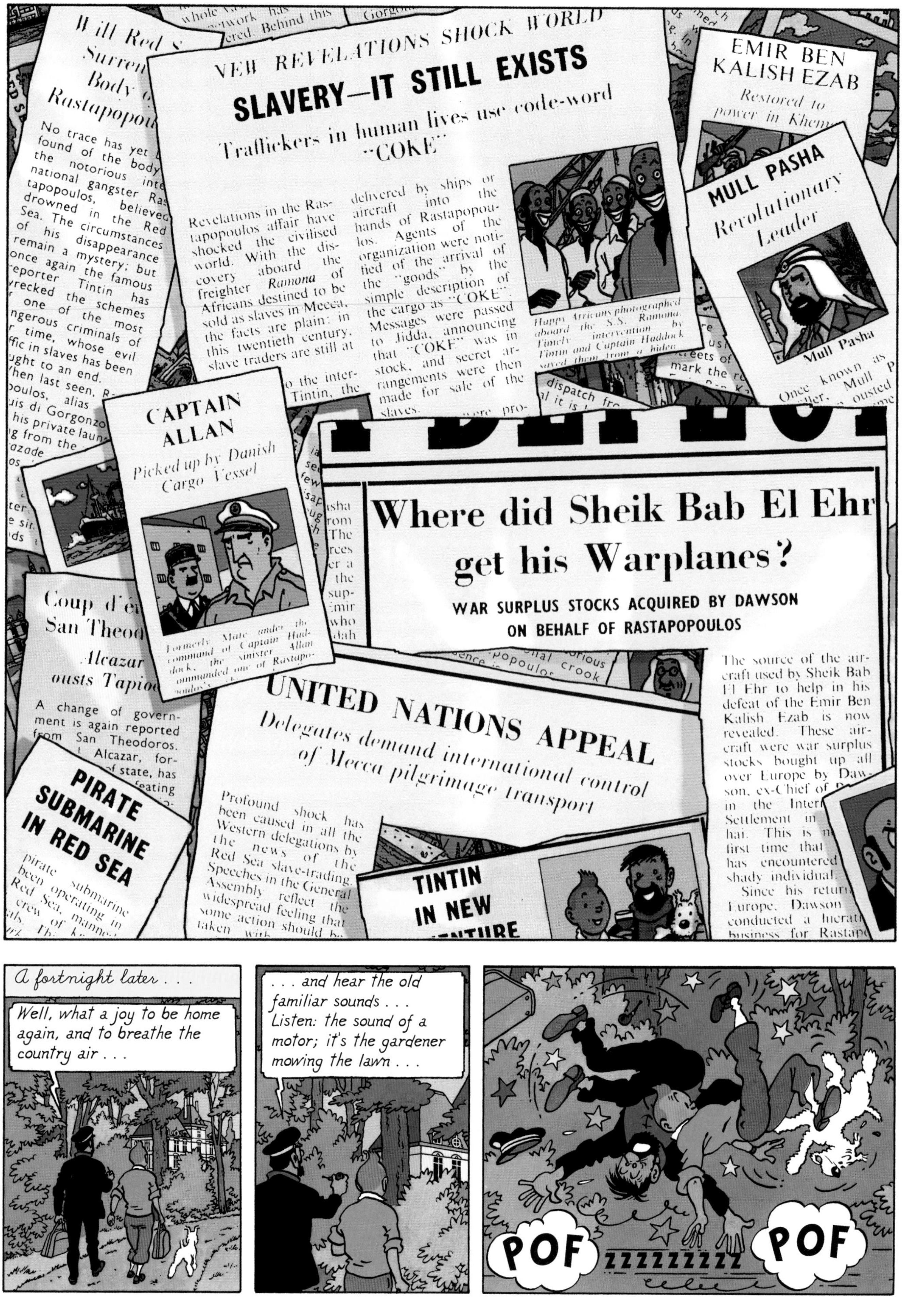
NEW REVELATIONS SHOCK WORLD
SLAVERY—IT STILL EXISTS
Traffickers in human lives use code-word "COKE"
Revelations in the Rastapopoulos affair have shocked the civilised world. With the discovery aboard the freighter Ramona of Africans destined to be sold as slaves in Mecca, the facts are plain: in this twentieth century, slave traders are still at
delivered by ships or aircraft into the hands of Rastapopoulos. Agents of the organization were notified of the arrival of the "goods" by the simple description of the cargo as "COKE". Messages were passed to Jidda, announcing that "COKE" was in stock, and secret arrangements were then made for sale of the slaves.
Happy Africans photographed aboard the S.S. Ramona. Timely intervention by Tintin and Captain Haddock
EMIR BEN KALISH EZAB
Restored to power in Khem
MULL PASHA
Revolutionary Leader
Mull Pasha
CAPTAIN ALLAN
Picked up by Danish Cargo Vessel
Where did Sheik Bab El Ehr get his Warplanes?
WAR SURPLUS STOCKS ACQUIRED BY DAWSON ON BEHALF OF RASTAPOPOULOS
The source of the aircraft used by Sheik Bab El Ehr to help in his defeat of the Emir Ben Kalish Ezab is now revealed. These aircraft were war surplus stocks bought up all over Europe by Dawson, ex-Chief of
UNITED NATIONS APPEAL
Delegates demand international control of Mecca pilgrimage transport
Profound shock has been caused in all the Western delegations by the news of the Red Sea slave-trading. Speeches in the General Assembly reflect the widespread feeling that some action should be
TINTIN IN NEW
Coup d'é
San Theod
Alcazar ousts Tapio
A change of government is again reported from San Theodoros.
PIRATE SUBMARINE IN RED SEA
No trace has yet been found of the body of the notorious international gangster Rastapopoulos, believed drowned in the Red Sea. The circumstances of his disappearance remain a mystery; but once again the famous reporter Tintin has wrecked the schemes of one of the most dangerous criminals of our time, whose evil traffic in slaves has been brought to an end.
A fortnight later . . .
Well, what a joy to be home again, and to breathe the country air . . .
. . . and hear the old familiar sounds . . . Listen: the sound of a motor; it's the gardener mowing the lawn . . .
POF
ZZZZZZZZZZ
POF

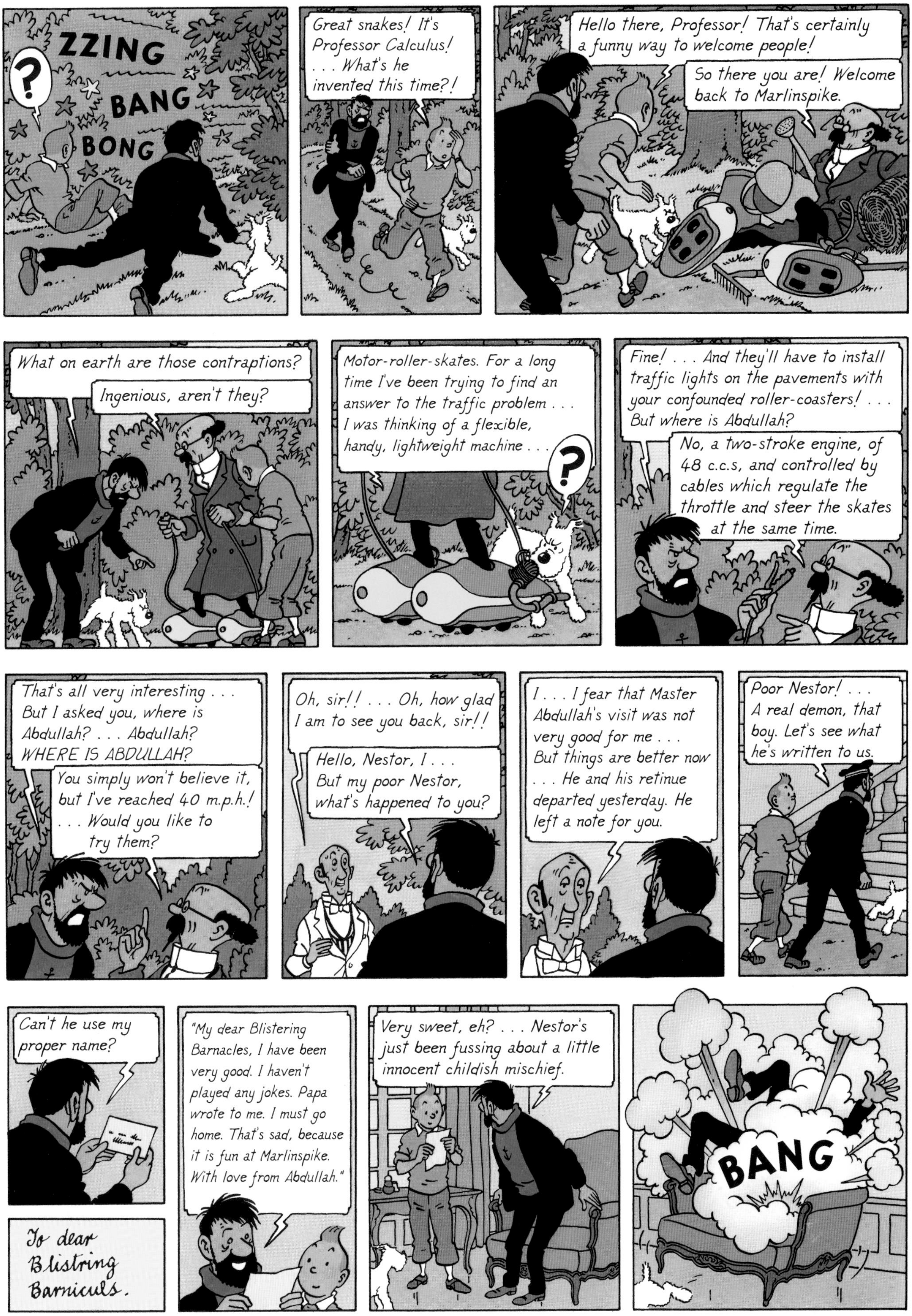
ZZING
BANG
BONG
?
Great snakes! It's Professor Calculus! . . . What's he invented this time?!
Hello there, Professor! That's certainly a funny way to welcome people!
So there you are! Welcome back to Marlinspike.
What on earth are those contraptions?
Ingenious, aren't they?
Motor-roller-skates. For a long time I've been trying to find an answer to the traffic problem . . . I was thinking of a flexible, handy, lightweight machine . . .
?
Fine! . . . And they'll have to install traffic lights on the pavements with your confounded roller-coasters! . . . But where is Abdullah?
No, a two-stroke engine, of 48 c.c.s, and controlled by cables which regulate the throttle and steer the skates at the same time.
That's all very interesting . . . But I asked you, where is Abdullah? . . . Abdullah? WHERE IS ABDULLAH?
You simply won't believe it, but I've reached 40 m.p.h.! . . . Would you like to try them?
Oh, sir!! . . . Oh, how glad I am to see you back, sir!!
Hello, Nestor, I . . . But my poor Nestor, what's happened to you?
I . . . I fear that Master Abdullah's visit was not very good for me . . . But things are better now . . . He and his retinue departed yesterday. He left a note for you.
Poor Nestor! . . . A real demon, that boy. Let's see what he's written to us.
Can't he use my proper name?
To dear Blistring Barniculs.
"My dear Blistering Barnacles, I have been very good. I haven't played any jokes. Papa wrote to me. I must go home. That's sad, because it is fun at Marlinspike. With love from Abdullah."
Very sweet, eh? . . . Nestor's just been fussing about a little innocent childish mischief.
BANG

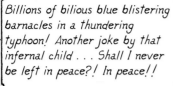

Billions of bilious blue blistering barnacles in a thundering typhoon! Another joke by that infernal child . . . Shall I never be left in peace?! In peace!!

Sir, Mr Wagg has just arrived . . .

Who? . . . Jolyon Wagg? . . . Oh, no, no! . . . I want some peace! . . . Peace!

Hello, old boy! How are you, you old sea-dog? I'm doing fine . . . in the pink! . . . Ha! ha! ha! . . . What a lark to see you again, you old humbug, you!

Er . . .

Well, my old salt, I've got a surprise for you . . . I know the country's pretty, but it's dull as ditchwater . . .

A matter of taste . . .

No, no, take it from me, it's dull. So I said to myself: "Jolyon," I said, "you must go and liven things up for that old stick-in-the-mud . . ."

That's very kind of you, but . . .

Now, now, turn it up! No buts! Too easy. I'm president of the Vagabond Car Club down my way; all I've had to do is organise a rally, and the final trials . . .

. . . are at Marlinspike!

CONTROL

START

THE END